RAVAGE

HELLISH #8

CHARITY PARKERSON

Ravage
Hellish #8
Charity Parkerson

--Warning: This book is intended for readers over the age of 18.

Editor: BZ Hercules & Consultants
ISBN: 978-1-946099-42-6

A human thrust into the world of the supernatural. The alpha mate who doesn't want him. It's all about to collide with the being who does.

Everything began with a stupid accident. As usual, Shepherd hadn't been paying attention when he sliced Raff's skin. His unwitting move left Raff scarred and revealed Shepherd's fate as the southeast pack leader's mate. It's a position he doesn't want.

Raff and Dante have been a couple for over fifty years. Despite knowing they aren't each other's fated mate, their love is strong and real. Until fate shows its hand, tearing them apart. Raff puts his foot down and refuses to claim Shepherd. Shepherd wants no part of being claimed. Meanwhile, Dante is trying his damnedest to lick his wounds and accept his loss. No one is coming out the winner in their standoff.

But when a demon comes calling, offering Shepherd a way to fix the damage he's caused, someone will have to break. Otherwise, they all might end up doomed.

ONE

THERE WERE EXACTLY NINE POINT SEVEN MILES between Jonathan's house and the Redwood motel where Shepherd stayed. Going by his watch and the space he'd already covered, Shepherd imagined it would take him around five hours to walk that far. That was fine. Not only could he make it before the sun rose, which mattered to the people he needed to see, he also needed the time to think. If his feet gave out, he'd call for a ride. Until then, he needed the peace. Not to mention, he needed to save his money for more important things—like to not be homeless.

Six months ago, Shepherd had been promoted to floor supervisor at the Flowood steel mill. Then heavy tariffs on steel hit them hard. Shepherd's entire line had been cut. Out of work and incapable of affording any type of life on unemployment, he'd accepted a job and a place to stay from his friend Raff. At the time, there'd already been a small part of him that knew it was a mistake. Turned out, it was so much bigger of a misstep than he could have dreamed. His life had never been great, but at least it had been his. Now, after a moment of stupid carelessness with a knife, not only was the world bigger than Shepherd ever dreamed, it seemed he was a wolf's mate. Yeah, fuck that.

It wasn't that Shepherd didn't like Raff. In fact, he liked Raff a little too much. He was the only reason Shepherd ever came to this parish. God knew it was nowhere near where he'd been living the last twelve years. Who in their right mind drove two hours to a place in the middle of nowhere to go to a bar? Exactly one person—Shepherd. The only person who'd ever questioned his sanity over the drive was his brother, Landry. Shepherd always shrugged and said he liked the atmosphere. Shepherd snorted. He didn't bother checking his surroundings to see if anyone heard. The trek to Jonathan's was in the middle of no fucking where. Shepherd kicked at the dirt, uncaring if at forty-one he looked like a petulant child. Fuck life. All it had ever done for him was give him shit, low self-esteem, and some horrible coping methods. The brush nearby crackled. Shepherd froze and eyed the tree line. Nothing. His nerves calmed. Raff had once warned him about the animals that would hunt at night in these areas. Shepherd shrugged it off and went back to making his way toward Jonathan's. He wasn't worried. They could eat him. No loss.

His mind wandered back to the night everything changed six months ago. He'd been promoted. There was nowhere else he wanted to be other than Raff's. His happiness had been too big. That was why he'd called his best friend Frankie and his baby brother, asking them to meet him at Raff's. He'd known he couldn't go alone. They'd been his shield from his feelings. Then, Raff and Dante had joined them. They'd pretended like they'd never met, protecting Shepherd's secret like they knew how he felt without him speaking. Shepherd had been too drunk. They'd sat too close. Of course, then Frankie had gotten all weird and disappeared, making the situation worse. Landry had run into a friend and hammered the final nail in Shepherd's coffin by abandoning him. He'd been alone with the pair.

Shepherd shook his head, trying to dislodge that night. It wouldn't leave. Flashes of Dante's emerald eyes, iridescent in the dark, slammed into Shepherd's mind. Phantom whispers filled his ears. His dick stirred. Shepherd's steps slowed until he stood on the shoulder of the road, staring at nothing. Seeing nothing but the images in his head. Visions of fangs piercing his skin and biting kisses. He couldn't breathe. Each labored breath came out sounding like a shot. Hyperventilating looked like a real possibility. His body wouldn't let that night go. It lived on his skin every second of the day.

Giving up, Shepherd dug out his phone and pulled up the app to hire a ride. He could still make the walk physically, but his mental state dissolved by the second. Shepherd hated himself too much to have this much time to think.

"Are you looking for me?"

In his surprise, Shepherd juggled his phone from hand to hand, doing his best to keep from dropping the device. God knew he couldn't afford to replace it. His heart pounded as he managed to snag the phone right before it hit the ground. When he glanced up, his heart hit double time. A man who lit up the night with his golden skin and also sported black wings hovered over him. His eyes swirled gold. He couldn't pass for human if he tried.

"Actually, I can," the man said, proving he could hear Shepherd's thoughts. "But my clothes fall off and sometimes my wings pop out for no reason or I have one green eye and one gold. It's just a hot mess." He shook his head. "I've given up fighting this form."

Shepherd blinked. "Did you just read my mind?"

The man-bird nodded. "Be glad you have loud thoughts, or you'd still be walking all night. Fortunately for you, I could hear your brain raging at me all the way to my house. I'm Jonathan. You're on your way to see me."

"Oh." Shepherd had never actually met Jonathan. He'd only heard people talk about him with awe. Being Raff's fated mate came with a few perks; no one had hesitated to tell him where he could find Jonathan. Of course, no one had told him Jonathan might find him. "Actually, you were only half of my plan. I also hoped to see Dante." From what he understood, Dante had accepted an invitation to stay with Jonathan after leaving Raff. Shepherd needed to speak his piece. First, he planned to beg for Jonathan's help. Then he'd beg for Dante's forgiveness, because that stupid accident with the knife had ruined the pair who'd given him the night of his dreams.

Jonathan scratched his chin and his eyes lost focus. "Nope. Dante still isn't home. I just checked. You coming with me or walking?"

5

"With you, I suppose." As the words left his lips, Shepherd questioned his sanity. All he had was the guy's word that he was Jonathan. With a mental shrug, he reached for Jonathan's outstretched hand. If he was being honest, he gave no fucks if he turned up dead in a ditch somewhere. At least then he wouldn't have to come up with this week's rent... and Dante and Raff could be together.

"You could always stay with me. I wouldn't charge you rent," Jonathan offered, reading his mind again. Before Shepherd could respond, the scenery changed, and he stood in the center of a gorgeous living area. The place was huge and obviously expensive. He tried looking in every direction without looking like he couldn't stop checking out the place. "Being the king has some perks—like having the space to take in long-term guests."

Shepherd wanted to be irritated over Jonathan's mind invasion, but he was too full of every other emotion to spare a brain cell for one more. "As it should, I'm sure." Being the king was probably a pain in the ass. After all, he was here to ask for help for something that probably meant nothing to Jonathan. If he had the nerve to do it, there were probably dozens of immortals lined up for help as well.

"We're about to have dinner soon. Would you

like to stay for that since I can see you don't want to stay with me?"

Shepherd rubbed his forehead. He didn't know how to deal with these people who constantly read his mind and could do all these things he couldn't. It was exhausting. "It's not that I don't want to stay. I don't know you or anyone, really. It would be awkward. I'd feel like an intruder."

"Plus, you're used to supporting yourself and not having a job is undermining your confidence."

"Exactly," Shepherd agreed. "I'd rather stay at the motel and keep my pride, even if I starve."

Jonathan's expression turned sad. "I know why you're here. As much as I'd love to tell you what you want to hear, I don't have the power to change my grandmother's mind. She fated you to be with Raff for a reason. I know you don't follow any particular faith, but just because you don't believe in her doesn't mean she doesn't believe in you. Goddess Celeste can see everything you can't. I can't force you to trust her, but you should. This happened for a reason."

In his heart, Shepherd had known no one would help him, especially someone from Raff's circle. He swallowed down the bitterness the way he always did. "Thank you for seeing me. If you'll point me toward the door, I'll be out of your hair."

"Eat and then I'll take you home."

Everything hurt. His chest. The backs of his eyes. All Shepherd wanted was to be free. "No." He tried softening his harsh tone. "Thank you, though."

"At least let me take you home."

Shepherd turned his back on Jonathan. He headed for a door that looked like it led outside. Since Jonathan had no trouble reading Shepherd's thoughts before now, Shepherd didn't see the point in continuing to argue. When he pulled open the door and the night air washed over him, Shepherd nearly sighed in relief. The air still smelled like freedom, even though his life was no longer his own.

"Dante doesn't blame you," Jonathan called out, stopping him.

Shepherd didn't look back. A heavy weight landed on his shoulders. He nearly buckled beneath the guilt. "I blame me," he muttered under his breath as he pulled the door closed behind him. Fifty years Dante and Raff had been together before Shepherd had come along and wrecked them. There was no forgiveness for that. Shepherd followed the weaving driveway through the trees, assuming it led to the road. When he found it, he pulled out his phone and opened his GPS. Shepherd had no idea where he was headed, but neither did he know where he was. He turned left, heading north. That seemed as good as anything. Even though Shepherd realized he was headed back toward the motel, he wasn't set on that destination. Maybe when he got there, he'd keep moving. There was nothing stopping him from walking and walking until he fell over in exhaustion. If no animals ate him, then he'd start again once he was rested. It wasn't the smart choice, but it was a choice. He hadn't been offered one of those in a while.

Shepherd barely made it twenty feet when a man popped out from the bushes. This time, it didn't startle him as much as Jonathan had. It was possible life had finally beaten him down too much for him to care. Jonathan had been his last hope. Now there was nothing except a long-ass walk in his future. The man's muscular arms were bare, but every other inch of him was covered by either his costume or elaborate makeup. He looked like one of the heavily painted voodoo priests that came out to play during the Day of the Dead celebrations. His face was white with black painted stitches around his lips. The man's completely black eyes were circled with black, making them seem like empty sockets. He even carried a walking stick and wore a top hat. He smiled at obviously having Shepherd's full attention.

"I sense you have a problem."

Shepherd snorted. "Doesn't everyone?"

He tried stepping around the stranger. Shepherd wasn't in the mood to deal with weirdos.

The guy leapt into his path, blocking him. "Ah, but you, my good Shepherd, I can feel all the blue. You're in luck. I'm just the being you need to make all your dreams come true." He dragged the handle of his walking stick down the center of Shepherd's chest as he made the claim. It was carved into an eerie-looking skull with red eyes.

The full impact of the man's words hit him. Shepherd froze in his tracks and eyed the man. "How do you know my name?"

The creepy black smile stretched into something dark and sinister. A chill raced up Shepherd's spine. "I know everything about you, Mr. LaTour. That is to be sure. You've been fated a mate you cannot escape. Luckily, I'm here to deal before it's too late."

Shepherd's head spun from all the rhymes. "Who are you?"

The stranger bowed. "I appear when you come to a crossroads in life. You, my good man, may call me Stryph."

Shepherd scrubbed at the back of his neck. He had all the alarms sounding, but he still couldn't simply walk away. This oddball was the first person to stand still and talk to him since his life blew to shreds who wasn't a part of Raff's inner circle. "Are you speaking in rhymes because you can't stop or because you're a clown?"

The man transformed, becoming a sexy blond-haired man. He looked exactly like a warrior Viking. His eyes were still completely black, but he wasn't as terrifying. "Would you rather I look this way? Does that make you feel better about me?"

"I don't know," Shepherd answered honestly. He'd been angry at life for so long, he no longer knew how he felt about anything. "You've stopped rhyming. That's all I care about."

Stryph smiled. It was blinding and scary at the same time. "Prose is important. Always remember that. Words and how they're strung together matter. They can change the course of history or leave you shattered." He planted his walking stick in the ground and did a small hop. Before Shepherd could growl his aggravation, Stryph winked. "Do you want me to take care of that little problem of you being mated to a wolf who doesn't want you?"

The hair stood on the back of Shepherd's neck.

"I have so many questions." Really, he did. Whoever Stryph was, he was obviously magical and well informed. "But I guess I should start with asking what you hope to gain in exchange for helping me?"

"I'm a demon."

Shepherd blinked. "Well, that doesn't sound good."

One side of Stryph's mouth lifted in a cocky smile. "I've already been more honest with you than anyone lately, have I not?"

He couldn't argue that point.

When he didn't respond, Stryph sighed. "A stab in the dark here—you don't know much about demons."

Shepherd scrubbed at his forehead. He had a headache that wouldn't quit. "I suppose I heard a thing or two in church growing up. Since then, I haven't taken much to religion. Too much hypocrisy, I suppose."

Stryph leaned on his walking stick. "I shall begin at the beginning, then. When Satan fell, one-third of the angels were cast down alongside him. Those were the first of my kind. I am a descendant of angels, except I'm not very angelic. In fact, some would call me greedy. I like things. All the things. Messy emotions and a sloppy existence. Everything people miss by walking the line. But I can't always have those things, because—as I said—I'm a demon. Only when I'm incorporeal and possessing another can I freely live the life I enjoy. Of course, I also like being me, so I wouldn't need you for long. Just on occasion."

"You want to possess me. That's not terrifying at all," Shepherd said dryly.

Stryph turned serious. "You realize I could just take you, right? A human is nothing to me, but I'd rather deal and have a willing mind merge with mine than listen to you scream." Stryph turned wicked. His expression screamed sex. "I promise you wouldn't regret anything. I'm not in the business of anything illegal, only carnal, and you were built for that." Stryph dropped his gaze to Shepherd's toes and openly inspected him before meeting his gaze again. "You see, it's a win-win. I get to enjoy a short jaunt of debauchery, keeping you completely safe, of course. You get the life you've always wanted." Stryph circled him. "What do you say, Mr. LaTour? Wouldn't you like to enjoy some time with someone who wants you? Aren't you tired of feeling like you're not good enough? I see inside your heart." Shepherd's heart sped. Stryph peeled away his layers, exposing his deepest fears and pain to the light. "You can't hide the hurt from me. I can see the way it slaughtered you when you realized you were good enough to fuck but not good enough to claim. Yet, you also don't want to be the home wrecker— like the man who stole your wife. In fact, if your giant wolf and sexy vampire stayed together and chose to keep you, you'd be—"

"Shepherd. Run." The shout cut off Stryph's painful speech and brought Shepherd's head around. Dante looked enraged as he sprinted toward Shepherd. Shepherd opened his mouth, intent on even he didn't know what, defending Stryph possibly. But Stryph turned to smoke, freezing the words on Shepherd's tongue. A gust of wind carried the demon away, leaving Shepherd alone with an enraged vampire.

"What the hell is wrong with you?" Dante barked.

Shepherd's throat unexpectedly swelled. That was a good question. He'd been wondering that same thing for as long as he could remember. What was so wrong with him that life continued kicking him at a constant? He never got to breathe or relax. It was always one horrible thing right after the other, stripping him away. Layer by layer, he was slowly disappearing. One day, there would be nothing left.

Dante's gaze moved over his features. "Are you okay? Did he touch you?"

Shepherd took a breath, trying to control the pain. "I'm fine," he lied, because he always did when asked that question. "He didn't touch me. He just wanted to make a deal."

"He just..." Dante seemed to flounder for a moment. "There is no just in making a deal with a demon. You're talking about your life. Your soul."

Shepherd shrugged. "Raff would be free, and you'd stop looking at me like you are right now. That's probably a fair trade."

Dante's expression snapped closed. Shepherd spent a moment staring at the hard features that had burrowed under his skin and led to his ruin. The long, dark hair. Emerald eyes that captured the light. Then Dante opened his mouth and his sexy accent—like an old English pirate—punched Shepherd in the gut as always. "You were dealing away your most precious possessions for Raff and me?"

Shepherd shook his head. "It's not for you if it's because I can't live with me."

Dante's eyes fell closed. When they reopened, Shepherd saw all the pain he caused staring out at him. All he felt was defeat. "Come on, poppet. I'll take you home."

"I don't have a home." Shepherd damn near choked on the words.

"As long as Raff lives, you'll have a home."

With one statement, the rage was back. This time, Shepherd kept it locked inside. Raff's place was an unwelcoming place to lay his head, one Shepherd didn't want. There was no sense in arguing. All these creatures could and would do as they pleased. Shepherd was nothing more than a helpless human, shifted around at their mercy. They'd turn their backs eventually, and Shepherd would break free again. Surely Stryph would find him again. Shepherd would deal. He had nothing to lose.

OUTRAGE OWNED DANTE. Shepherd had no clue what horrors he'd narrowly escaped. But it wasn't Shepherd who would feel Dante's wrath. Shepherd wasn't to blame for any of this. Raff should be taking care of his mate. Dante had walked away, leaving the stupid wolf free to care for Shepherd without Dante standing in the way. His sacrifice had obviously been for nothing. More than that. Raff's refusal to claim his mate was like spitting in the face of Dante's sacrifice.

Dante took Shepherd's hand. Even though Shepherd didn't fight him, Dante felt his determination. He didn't want to go back to Raff. That was too damn bad. They were mates, and they'd be fucking happy, because Dante had lost every goddamn thing so they could be.

In an instant, they were inside Raff's cabin. Since Raff had spent the last fifty years with Dante, he didn't normally look the least bit surprised to see Dante when he magically appeared out of nowhere. Today was no different. Dante's rage wasn't helped by the sight of Raff. His hairy barrel chest and deep cut abs were bare for Dante to eat alive with his gaze. In nothing but jeans that were unbuttoned at the waist, Raff held a cup of coffee in one hand and his phone in the other. Dante had obviously caught him on his way to the couch.

"Did you need something, babe?" Raff asked, as if this was a social call.

Dante rolled his tongue back in and took some breaths. Even half a century together hadn't cooled his reaction to the sexy alpha. "No. I'm returning your wayward mate."

Raff's amber gaze slid Shepherd's way. Shepherd stared in the other direction, visibly trying to hide the waves of pain rolling off him. "He isn't wayward. I imagine he was doing exactly as he pleased when you found him—like the adult that he is."

A small smile touched Shepherd's lips. Dante felt the hum of satisfaction inside Raff over pleasing his mate. He wanted to die. This was hell for him and no one noticed they were slowly killing him.

"Whatever. You're welcome. He's home now."

"I don't live here," Shepherd muttered while keeping his gaze averted. "I live at the Redwood Motel."

"Nobody lives at a motel. It's a motel, for fuck's sake," Dante barked, getting sick of the ungratefulness after saving Shepherd from a demon. He took another breath and focused on Raff. "May I speak to you alone?"

He didn't miss the hope mixed with pain that crossed Raff's features as he set his phone and coffee aside. With a nod, Raff headed for the bedroom. Dante followed. Shepherd still stood only feet away. Dante chose to ignore that fact for a moment as he focused on Raff.

"Why isn't he living here?"

"I'm right here," Shepherd said, sounding tired. "You could ask me. This isn't my home. It's yours. I don't belong here. You do."

Dante chose to continue ignoring Shepherd

since he wasn't over being pissed off about the situation he'd found the man in. "He should be here, Raff. You can't keep him safe if you're under different roofs."

In a move obviously intended to enrage Dante, Raff raked Dante's body with his gaze. Heat stroked him, weakening Dante's knees. Damn. He missed his wolf. "Once again, Shepherd is a grown man. He's not my child. If he wants to stay here, he's welcome. If he doesn't, I won't chain him to a chair."

"You don't chain children either," Dante said, getting sidetracked and hearing the horror in his voice before shaking it away. He knew Raff was trying to get under his skin. "I shouldn't have to go looking for your mate because he's out walking in the middle of the night," Dante growled, getting back on topic.

"No one asked you to," Shepherd called out, making things worse.

Dante snapped. "Do you know where I found him?" Dante yelled as he slammed the bedroom door, shutting Shepherd out of the conversation. "He was trying to bargain away his soul so we can be together." Dante motioned between them, trying to impress the seriousness of the situation upon Raff. In the past fifty years, he'd been angry with Raff more times than he could count, but this was a whole new level of fury. They'd always known Raff would find his true mate one day. Dante had always known it would hurt. He'd never in a million years expected Raff to turn his back on his mate when it happened. This was one place they didn't get a choice. Goddess Celeste made those decisions. Some of the air left his sails. The fight went out of him. "What are you doing, Raff? This guy is your mate. It's your duty to keep him safe."

The stubborn tilt to Raff's jaw never wavered. "As I said, I can't force him to accept me or stay here. That's a sentiment I would think you'd understand. After all, this is your home too and you refuse to stay. We have a life together, Dante," Raff said, his tone turning pained. "You just walked away from it."

It was a knife to his heart every time he set eyes on Raff. This was the little slice of heaven they'd shared. Maybe in a hundred years, he'd feel different. But today, standing here in what used to be their bedroom, everything hurt. "Could you still love me, knowing I stood in the way of the life Goddess Celeste chose for you?"

Raff moved closer until they were chest to chest. "Yes. I would still love you no matter what. Even if I found out tomorrow that you're some crazed serial killer, you'd still be the greatest love of my life. He doesn't want me. I thought that you did. Stay."

Dante swallowed past the pain and the desire to close the final inch between them. Missing Raff's kiss was like a hot poker in his gut. "Maybe you're okay with that scenario, but I wouldn't like me if I stayed. And I can't respect someone who'd allow their mate to bargain away everything they have, because you were being selfish. He doesn't understand. This isn't his world. Do you honestly think he doesn't feel that you're still trying to work things out with me? No wonder he doesn't want to you. He doesn't realize why your rejection cuts twice as deep as anything he's ever experienced. Maybe you're okay with that, but I'm not. I guess, until you're ready to accept things, I'll do my best to watch out for Shepherd." Dante shook his head. Each passing moment, the pain increased. The choking sensation worsened. He headed for the door. "I never thought I'd see the day when you'd hurt me like this by leaving me the responsibility of the man who took my place."

Raff tried reaching for him. Dante dissipated before their skin collided, reappearing at the door. He couldn't take Raff touching him. It might be the thing that broke him.

"Dante, please?"

Dante opened the door, incapable of enduring another second in their bedroom. The living room was empty. "Fuck me," Dante growled. He concentrated on Shepherd's location. He was in the backseat of an Uber and on his way back to Jonathan's. No doubt he was looking for the demon. Goddamn it. Dante let Raff's cabin fall away. He appeared in the backseat of the SUV with Shepherd. He didn't look Shepherd's way as he touched the driver's shoulder. "You do not see us or hear us. We were never here. Just keep driving."

A loud sigh filled the backseat. "Please go away, Dante. Just go back to Raff. Don't think about me again, and I'll make this right."

Dante's spine molded to the seat. He wanted to hate Shepherd. It was impossible. The man was just too damn nice and selfless. He was also a fool. "What kind of person do you think I am? Do you really think I could skip away and pretend you're not living in hell with a demon while I go back to my life?"

Shepherd's gaze slid Dante's way. Fury blazed in his eyes. "What kind of person do *you* think *I* am? Do you think I can go back to Raff's, warm the bed you shared with him, and forget I ruined your life? That's not me. I can't be that guy. That guy ruined my life years ago while I was off fighting for my country. I can't be that person." The rage filling every word Shepherd spoke hit Dante in the chest. In that moment, he realized Shepherd really meant it. He would trade himself for Dante's happiness.

"Take a breath, Shepherd. Calm down."

An ugly-sounding snort escaped Shepherd. "Has anyone ever calmed down in the history of being told to calm down? I'm pissed off, Dante. Your God isn't mine. I don't follow her rules."

"People calm down when I tell them to," Dante said, sounding petulant even to his ears as Shepherd ignored him and kept talking.

Shepherd poked himself in the chest. "I don't have to do anything. This is my life. I've spent the whole of it miserable. So if I want to spend the rest of eternity that way, it's my damn business. Not yours. Not Raff's. Not your goddamn Goddess Ce—"

Dante kissed him. He didn't know how else to make the venomous speech stop. For some reason he couldn't explain, Shepherd was impervious to Dante's mind control. He should've calmed the second Dante told him to do so. This was the only weapon Dante possessed—Shepherd's desire for him. Dante put every ounce of skill he had into their kiss. He curled his tongue around Shepherd's and stroked. The scent of Shepherd's lust filled the car.

His reasons for touching Shepherd slipped away. He shaped Shepherd's erection through his jeans and massaged him. Shepherd's hips left the seat, seeking more. Memories crowded his brain. Hurt made him want to turn a blind eye to the truth. In these moments, the moments when they touched, Dante couldn't lie to himself. His feelings for Shepherd rose to the surface and choked him.

Dante pulled away and pressed his forehead to Shepherd's. He held the man's stare as he stroked him. "Do you ever think of that night?" Dante didn't wait for Shepherd to answer. He could see inside Shepherd's head. All the memories were there. "I wanted you every bit as much as you wanted us. Stop telling yourself you trespassed in our relationship. We invited you in. I am five hundred years old. Trust me. I'm old enough to know when I want someone." He recaptured Shepherd's lips before the man could find a new argument. Shepherd wouldn't sell his life or soul on Dante's watch. Maybe Raff could conveniently forget they'd been the ones to seduce Shepherd, but Dante couldn't. This human was their responsibility. They'd dragged him into their world with their inability to deny themselves pleasure. Raff had thought of Shepherd as a friend once upon a time. Dante had thought him more than a friend.

Shepherd wasn't their enemy. This wasn't his fault. Goddamn, he still tasted like unadulterated lust just as he had that night.

Dante's fangs grew. Shepherd didn't back down. If anything, he kissed Dante deeper, as if begging for Dante to do his worst. Dante's dick leaked in his pants like Shepherd's tongue stroked it. Every ounce of anger and bitterness fell away. Dante knew it would be back, but—for now—he reveled in the reprieve.

Riskel. Dante put out the mental call. He still needed to fix this.

Dante? What's wrong?

Do you have room for a guest? A demon has caught my friend's scent. He isn't safe.

Of course. Dante had known he could count on Risk. *With me staying with Jonathan until Tamil finishes his magic training or feels comfortable enough to leave, the house is empty. Make yourself at home. The place is completely warded against demons.*

Dante never lost his focus on Shepherd. *Thank you, my friend.* As he closed his mind to all others, Dante slid Shepherd's zipper down. His fingers encircled Shepherd's cock, setting him free. He stroked as he kissed his way down Shepherd's massive chest. Damn, the guy was built like a bull in every way. Dante wasn't used to denying himself. He felt Shepherd's slight reluctance now that they were no longer kissing. Dante dropped his head and licked away Shepherd's pre-cum, killing all doubt. A moan filled the car. Dante took Shepherd down his throat. He didn't need air the way a human did. Shepherd could fuck his throat all day. The way Shepherd held his hair and pumped against Dante's mouth made Dante proud. Shepherd might be human, but he was strong. Dante loved strong men. He craved the rough treatment. When he felt someone's touch even after they were gone, that was when Dante felt his most powerful. Shepherd didn't disappoint. He used Dante, openly taking his pleasure. Shepherd moaned and thrust. He pulled Dante's hair and beat at the back of his throat.

"Fuck. You're amazing. Don't stop." Shepherd sucked in an audible breath. "I've thought about you doing this every night since we were together. You're fucking perfect."

With each word of praise, Dante tried harder to please Shepherd. He licked and sucked. When hot cum flooded Dante's mouth, satisfaction roared through him. The instant he'd licked Shepherd dry, he straddled the man's lap. He buried his face against

Shepherd's throat, smelling his blood. It called to him. He could hear Shepherd's steady pulse.

Shepherd hugged him, drawing him closer. "It's yours. Take it."

Dante's fangs sank into Shepherd's vein before permission died on Shepherd's lips. Shepherd's hips lifted as if he tried burying himself in Dante's ass as the first pull of blood left his body. Fuck. Dante wanted that, but he couldn't, because that meant letting Raff go. A wave of sadness washed over Dante, reminding him of everything he'd lost. Shepherd's tight hold turned into a caress, as if he felt Dante's hurt.

"Let me give him back," Shepherd begged, sounding every bit as hurt.

Shepherd didn't understand. He couldn't. Goddess Celeste's decisions were absolute. It wasn't possible to defy a god. Not even a demon could deal away fate.

Dante licked Shepherd's throat, healing the puncture wounds. "Let me take you somewhere you can get away. You'll have a free roof over your head and no one will be there, making you feel pressured to make any decisions. Just breathe for a little while."

Shepherd's pain overwhelmed Dante, forcing him to close his mind to Shepherd to save his sanity.

"I have bills to pay. As much as I'd like to take some time away from reality, I need to be out searching for a way to support myself."

Actually, he didn't. Whether Shepherd accepted him or not, Raff was his mate. It was Raff's job to take care of Shepherd. Dante knew Shepherd didn't want to hear that right now, but he couldn't back down. There was still a demon out there.

"Don't worry over that." He straightened Shepherd's clothes and dissipated, taking Shepherd along for the ride. He landed on Risk's front steps. The place was quiet. "This is my friend's place. He's currently away on business."

Shepherd turned in a circle, eyeing their surroundings. Dante knew what he saw. Riskel's property had once been a lucrative sugar plantation. The only realistic way in or out was by boat or immortal means. A person could walk through miles of forest to the nearest road, but no roads led to the plantation. It was in the middle of nowhere. That didn't mean the place wasn't amazing. In fact, the main house was so large Dante had never seen inside every room.

"Wow."

Dante nodded. "This place is the perfect spot to hide from your problems. Risk and his husband

Tamil are staying with the king for a while, so it'll be just you. I'll bring you some food and whatnot. You don't have to stay long, if you don't want, but stay a few days, please, poppet?" Just long enough for the demon to get bored and move on. Long enough for Raff to worry and come for him. Just long enough for Dante to disappear and start over someplace new.

Shepherd headed for the door. "Should I just go in? Is it unlocked?"

Relief poured through Dante. "Yeah. This place is protected by powerful magic. It's not possible for anyone to break in or sneak past the warding. You'll be safe."

Shepherd opened the door but didn't immediately go inside. Instead, he stared at the horizon over Dante's shoulder as if he couldn't bring himself to look directly at Dante. Dante stole the chance to stare at Shepherd freely. His eyes were an amazing shade of green. He was such a beautiful man. Dante rubbed his chest. Shepherd made him feel things he couldn't explain.

"You don't have to stay. I can feel how much it's hurting you to look at me."

The breath entering Dante's lungs stuttered. He wanted to lie and say it wasn't true. It wasn't like Shepherd meant for any of this to happen. "I'll come by sometime early tomorrow evening with some supplies. Until then, you should get some sleep. You're not used to keeping our hours."

Shepherd nodded. He still didn't look Dante's way. Dante closed the distance between them and touched his lips to Shepherd's. He could no more stop himself than he could stop Shepherd from being Raff's mate. He held Shepherd's bottom lip between his teeth as he let the surroundings disappear. Dante reappeared at the edge of the king's property. As he made the trek up the winding driveway, Dante told himself he'd do better tomorrow. He'd drop some supplies off with Shepherd and then he'd leave. He could go anywhere in the world. Maybe he'd head to France or Sweden. There were tons of beautiful Swedish men. Right now, he didn't want to look at anyone, especially himself. He was quickly losing his desire to keep going. Maybe he wouldn't. No one said he had to.

TWO

THERE WASN'T A SINGLE CHANCE IN HELL
Shepherd could sleep in a stranger's home. He'd
spent close to an hour migrating from room to room,
trying to find peace. There was none to be had. The
whole house looked like something out of a magazine
or a storybook. There was china in the dining room
that looked like it cost more than Shepherd's entire
life. The living room looked more like a study with
its countless books. There wasn't a TV or a
computer. As far as Shepherd could tell, there was
no access to the outside world whatsoever. That
included the outside of the house as well.

When Shepherd had tired of searching for
comfort indoors, and the sun began to rise, he'd
started a tour of the grounds. There were paths that

led to more paths, which led to outbuildings. Not a single trail led to a road. With each passing minute, Shepherd's frustration grew. Just when he almost lost all hope, he spotted Stryph. The man or demon or whatever he was drew a line in the brush with his foot. He never looked Shepherd's way as he approached. Stryph's dark gaze wasn't dark in the daylight. His eyes were the lightest gray Shepherd had ever seen. Stryph looked in every direction, as if seeing something Shepherd couldn't before making the line in the brush and grass longer. Shepherd stopped feet away and watched while waiting for Stryph to acknowledge him.

"I can't see you," Stryph finally said. "This place is surrounded by a bubble of strong magic. Here," he said, toeing the ground and making the line even longer. "Even though I can't see you, I know you're there. I can feel you just out of reach."

"That's odd. I can see you."

Stryph's face lit. "Ah. I knew you were there."

"Funny that you can hear me, but you can't see me."

"I don't know," Stryph said, sounding thoughtful. "I suppose whoever the voodooist was that created this bubble thought there was no harm in chatting with demons as long as they couldn't touch. In truth, it's a smart move. If you don't like what you hear, you can move along. They can't chase you or harm you inside your magic ball."

Shepherd found it odd that Stryph kept talking about demons as if they were a group he didn't consider himself a part of. Everything was "they" and "them" rather than "we" and "us." "What are you doing?"

Stryph kept making his line longer. "I'm mapping the edge of the magic. That way, you'll know where you're safe and how to get to me."

"Are you saying I'm not safe if I cross the line?" For some reason Shepherd couldn't explain, he was enjoying himself. Maybe it was because he could do whatever and Stryph couldn't harm him, or maybe his mind had finally snapped. Either way, he didn't have the slightest desire to return to the house.

Devilry lit Stryph's eyes, making them iridescent. "I guess you won't know until you do. Come on, Shepherd. Be bad with me. Aren't you tired of behaving? All you have to do is step over the line and I'll set you free."

He was exhausted. Even Shepherd's stress had stress. He didn't want to be good anymore. What had that ever gotten him? Exactly nothing. Shepherd stepped over the line before he could talk himself into being the goddamn adult another day.

Stryph's smile turned wicked as he caught sight of Shepherd. "Are you ready to be someone new?"

"Tell me why you want me first." Fuck. It was like he was incapable of letting go.

"You're perfect." Those two words were like a healing balm on Shepherd's wounded soul. Stryph didn't stop there. "Not only are you beautiful, you don't care about color or genders. You're intellectually and sexually appealing in every way. Let's have some fun."

"Okay." God help him. His agreement was out there before he could change his mind.

Stryph's smile alone made the agreement worthwhile. Shepherd wondered what it said about him that a demon was the only person he'd made happy in a long damn time. Stryph turned to smoke. "You won't regret me." The smoke overcame him, stealing Shepherd's breath. Then it was over. He was there, but he wasn't. Shepherd still had all his senses, but he wasn't in the driver's seat. "Mhmm. I can't wait to get you home." The words came from Shepherd's mouth, but they didn't come from him. His hands lifted and ran down his body. "Oh, we're definitely going for a test drive very soon, but first, let's stop by and see that naughty alpha."

What? Raff? Why are we going to see Raff? I thought you said you'd remove the mating thing or whatever.

"Oh, sweetie. That's not what I said. No one can undo fate. That's a whole other department from mine. Remember what we discussed about prose? I said I could make all your dreams come true, and I will. Just let me put my expertise to work. Relax. Enjoy the ride. Papa Stryph will make your life aces."

A growl sounded in Shepherd's head, but Stryph used his lips to chuckle. His feet moved. It was as if all Shepherd could do was watch as everything happened to him. He concentrated on breathing. They had a deal. Shepherd would honor his half and pray Stryph did the same. It seemed as if they walked forever before coming to a road. On the shoulder sat a black Bugatti Chiron. The windows were tinted too dark to see inside. The doors unlocked as they approached and Stryph slid behind the wheel. Shepherd realized he still had some control as he eyed the inside of the car in awe. It was obviously new. Shepherd hadn't owned anything new or nice in as long as he could remember. He'd certainly never been inside a car that cost more than he'd ever made in all his years of working put together.

"I've got you, sexy. Royalty has its perks."

Did you say royalty?

"Does it matter? I only meant I can afford to show you the best time you've ever had, but first things first. Let's make Raff sweat." Stryph floored it, hitting speeds that should have terrified Shepherd, but he was fairly certain he couldn't die as long as Stryph was in control. The car hugged the curves. Laughter filled the car. Shepherd didn't know if it came from him or Stryph. It didn't matter. He felt... free. It was like air fully inflated his lungs for the first time in years. Shepherd hadn't realized how bad things were until Stryph released his chains.

At Raff's Pool Hall, Stryph backed into a parking space a distance from the door. It seemed an odd choice to Shepherd, but he assumed Stryph didn't want his car to get dinged.

"Let's stir this shit pot," Stryph said, leaping from the car. As they cleared the door, Shepherd could feel the eyes upon him. He wanted to look for Raff. The desire was crippling. Stryph intentionally kept him from doing so. Instead, he headed for the first empty pool table. Before he could feel Shepherd's pockets and discover exactly how broke Shepherd was, Raff's chest collided with his back. Shepherd felt Stryph's satisfaction roar.

"What are you doing here, Shepherd?"

His head didn't turn. "Killing time." Damn. Shepherd was impressed with how unconcerned he sounded.

Raff's nose touched his throat. "Why do you smell different?"

Fucker. He doesn't want me. Why is he sniffing me? Since Stryph was in control, Shepherd's mouth didn't say any of the things he wanted. Instead, his shoulders lifted in a careless shrug. "Probably because I've been out in the swamp, staying with Risk."

Raff's hands found Shepherd's hips, as if he couldn't resist touching him. He massaged. Shepherd got the impression the move was an unconscious one. "Seriously, Shep. Why are you here? I thought you were doing your best to stay away. Hell, you even quit, knowing you have no way to pay your bills, just to get away from me."

"I came to tell you I'm going away." He turned and finally met Raff's sexy amber gaze. Inside, Shepherd whimpered. Outside, Stryph slayed.

"Promise me you'll do your damnedest to win Dante back, and you'll never see me again."

Raff didn't smile. In fact, he looked pinched, as if there wasn't enough air. "Where are you going?"

Shepherd shook his head. "Just away. You haven't claimed me, so there's nothing binding us, right? I want you to be with Dante. It's best if I go." Without another word, Shepherd gave Raff a sharp nod and stepped around him, headed for the door. He felt Raff follow. Stryph's satisfaction grew.

"I'd feel better if you would at least tell me where you'll be."

Shepherd didn't look back. "Bye, Raff."

As they made their way to the car, he could feel Raff's stare. The car started and Stryph hopped into the passenger side.

What are we doing?

Stryph cackled as he twisted and climbed over the console and into the driver's seat, impressing Shepherd with a dexterity he never would've believed he possessed. "The windows are too dark for him to see. He thinks you just got into some rich dude's car. Technically, you did, but still." Stryph pulled from the lot, still laughing. "Oh, babe. I don't know what you're thinking. He wants you. In fact, he wants you so bad it's eating him alive. Now you've added some mystery and jealousy to an alpha's pot. Pretty soon, he'll come running."

I don't want him to come running. He's supposed to be with Dante.

"All good things in time, sexy. Have a little faith in me. Now I first intend to spoil you a little and then I plan to soil you a lot. Let's hit the town."

Shepherd settled in inside his own mind while Stryph drove. The incident with Raff felt different. Maybe it was because he'd gotten to experience the moment as an outsider. Raff had wanted him. Shepherd felt it. He wished that made things less complicated. Instead, the knowledge simply mixed with his confusion to further muddy the waters. By the time Shepherd let the topic go and looked around, he no longer recognized the scenery. Everything was upper class. Every building was close together and at least five floors high, but all the buildings looked to be made of old stone—like they'd slid into a place filled with old money. It was odd. They hadn't been driving that long, yet Shepherd didn't have a clue where they were. He'd grown up in New Orleans. He'd never been here.

Where are we?

"This is my town." He parallel parked in front of one of the buildings. Someone opened the door for them. Stryph headed for the door without looking back. Once again, the door to the building opened ahead of them, anticipating Stryph's every move.

A small elderly man bustled their way. "Mr. Stryph. It's always a pleasure."

How did he know that you're you?

Stryph ignored Shepherd. "Hello, Dagon. You're looking well. As you can see, I've acquired a new playmate. He's the casual sort, so I hate to change what makes him so handsomely unique. So I'll be needing something expensive yet unfussy. I'd say ten outfits should do it. The works, please."

"Of course, sir."

Stryph stood still while the old man took quick measurements. Shepherd couldn't stop trying to look in every direction. Everything was dark wood and marble with shitty but expensive-looking lighting. There were mirrors, but they were empty of reflections, which was surreal as fuck since there was literally not a single reason for Shepherd not to have a reflection.

With the measurements out of the way, Stryph headed back toward the door. "Have everything delivered by the end of the day, please. I'm eager to get this one home."

"Of course, Mr. Stryph." The words were called

at their back as Stryph made his way back to the car. The door stood open and waiting.

Shepherd didn't bother with more questions. He was too busy trying to see everything that Stryph refused to look at. After two blocks, Stryph turned down a drive between two buildings and circled the gray stone townhome before parking in the back.

"This is my home."

It's fucking amazing. Shepherd couldn't contain his reaction and they hadn't even gone inside yet. The place was five floors—like every other building. Even the windows looked expensive. As they cleared the door, all Shepherd smelled was wood. Polished wood. Everything had an odd hue. The same as the shop—like every place was badly lit. Shepherd didn't think it was due to being possessed. Raff's hadn't looked like this. The oddness of the lighting lost its importance under the disbelief of how beautiful everything was everywhere he looked. Shepherd didn't know much about antiques, but he could tell every stick of furniture was made of real wood, obviously made in the days when things had been built to last. No particle board bullshit here. He didn't get to inspect much of anything before Stryph jogged up a flight of stairs and stepped into a bedroom that took up one entire floor of the building.

It was open. One wall was solid wood shelves and rods—like an open closet. A gigantic four poster bed was the focal point of the room with deep maroon coverings. He could see a bathroom through the only doorway.

Jesus. This place is... wow.

Stryph chuckled. "Don't bring Jesus into it. He was a pauper, and a bit of a hippie. There's nothing inexpensive about this place." Stryph walked to a full-length mirror and stared at Shepherd's reflection. "But nothing I own compares to the prize I just brought home. Look at you."

Shepherd saw himself all the time. That was nothing new. He wasn't impressed. *Why can I see my reflection here while I couldn't at that shop?*

Stryph took off his shirt. "Not every mirror is a mirror. Sometimes, they are doors. Damn, Shepherd. You're gorgeous."

The heat in Stryph's tone had Shepherd focusing on the moment. He really looked at his reflection. His eyes were different. It was Stryph staring back at him. He felt the man's desire.

Thank you. He meant it. No one had truly made him feel sexy in a long time.

"It's time for that test drive. I like to know what I'm buying. How much can you take?"

Um. Shepherd suddenly felt in deep. *How do you mean?*

His hands went to the button of his jeans. "I need to know what this body can endure. What brings you pleasure? At what point does ecstasy turn to pain for you?"

It was insane. Realistically, Shepherd understood he was looking at himself, but he couldn't recall the last time he'd felt so desired. He wanted to be touched. Shepherd watched as Stryph stripped the clothes from him. He was hard, and even Shepherd didn't know if it was his lust or Stryph's driving him.

"Do you even know yourself, Shepherd? Look. See how strong you are all on your own. Your worth has never been defined by others." He stroked his cock. Pleasure rocked him. "Do you really believe you need an alpha to make you whole? You've always already been complete. Let me show you."

Shepherd's chest felt full. It had been ages since anyone made him feel important. Life had been one huge blow to his ego and heart for too long.

"I should show you my bathroom. Let's do that. It's pretty badass."

It wasn't as if Shepherd had much choice. His feet moved, carrying him inside the bathroom. The room was badass. He'd never seen a shower with so much stuff. It didn't even look like a shower any longer. The large area with all the shower heads, nozzles, massagers, and spouts looked like some sort of specialized power cleaning device. Shepherd was used to a regular shower, one where he stepped over the edge of the bathtub and it had one head. He was tall, so those kind of sucked, but it had been that way his whole life. This bathroom had a separate tub that looked like it would seat eight people.

I'd hate to pay your water bill.

Stryph laughed. "You worry over the oddest details. Someone like me doesn't pay for anything. I take what I deserve. What would you have if you could reach out and take it without restrictions?"

Happiness. Shepherd didn't even need to think about it. If life gave him one wish, no limitations, he'd choose happiness every time.

"You already have everything you need to reach out and grab that one," Stryph said as he turned the water on in the bathtub. "Take what you want, Shepherd. Don't wait for anyone to give you what you're owed." Steam filled the air. Stryph started the jets on the tub and poured something sweet-smelling into the water. Shepherd's hands moved down his body, caressing every line. "This is your weapon. Use it." Stryph stepped into the tub, sinking into the water. The jets hit at all the perfect angles. A groan escaped Shepherd, sounding loud as it vibrated off the walls of the bathroom. Shepherd didn't know if it came from him or Stryph. "Humans feel everything so much stronger than immortals. We're more immune to injury, but some sensation is lost to us in the process. But humans, fuck," Stryph said, using Shepherd's hands to stroke him. "You feel everything."

After leaning his head back against the tub's edge, Stryph closed his eyes, blinding Shepherd. He was trapped inside the darkness with nothing left to him except the sensation of Stryph's touch. It was truly as if someone else was touching him. Shepherd tried opening his eyes. Nothing happened.

"Don't watch. Just enjoy. I'll take care of you."

Shepherd tried to relax, but an odd pang of guilt tried sneaking in. Stryph wasn't Raff or Dante. He didn't think anyone else should be touching him.

"Technically, you're touching yourself. Stop overthinking things, sexy. But it's funny how you included Dante in the equation, don't you think?"

Not really. Shepherd didn't even have to think it over. He was the intruder in the Dante and Raff equation.

"If you're the intruder, then I'm not trespassing."

This time, the words came from Stryph's lips and caressed Shepherd's ears. A solid weight settled across his hips a half second before a hot mouth covered his. Shepherd's thoughts scattered. He automatically opened, oddly desperate to taste the man who'd occupied him only seconds earlier. Their kiss was deep and filled with madness. Shepherd tugged Stryph's hair, dragging him closer and manhandling him in his crazed haze. Stryph's fingernails scored Shepherd's skin, digging deep. He bit hard enough to draw blood from Shepherd's bottom lip. Stryph sucked. Shepherd's cock jumped as if it was happening to his dick.

Stryph's voice filled his head. *Sleep, Shepherd. You won't want to see what comes next.*

"What?" Everything went black before his question was answered.

Shepherd's eyes popped open. He stood at a bar, eyeing a large man nearby.

"You're so defiant. Sleep, Shepherd." He tried, but the noise kept him from completely detaching. Music thrummed in his ears. Light flashed like a strobe, even with his lids closed. His clothes felt soft. He opened his eyes and looked down at himself. The jeans and t-shirt covering his body didn't look familiar. *Whose clothes am I wearing?*

"The new ones I bought for you. Now sleep, Shepherd."

His eyes opened again without thought. Leather filled his hand. A whip zipped through the air before biting into the flesh of the nude man who was chained spread eagle in the center of the room. Blood pooled across the man's back.

"Sleep, Shepherd."

Once again, his eyes felt too heavy to hold open. Music and moans cut through the darkness. More flashes of light brought his vision to life again. Sweat coated his skin. Pain and ecstasy collided as bodies writhed around him. He pumped inside someone. Shepherd couldn't see their face.

"Sleep, Shepherd."

This time, at Stryph's commanding tone, there was nothing but an inky void of blackness and peace.

THREE

THE SICK FEELING IN RAFF'S GUT WOULDN'T LET go. Shepherd hadn't looked the least bit hurt as he'd dropped the news he was going away. Who had he left with? Raff rubbed his chest. Everything was fucked up. Goddamn it. It wasn't that he didn't want his mate. He did. Everything inside him pulled him toward Shepherd. Things weren't that cut and dry. He knew he couldn't fight fate forever. Neither could he claim Goddess Celeste hadn't chosen him a strong mate. It was beyond obvious Shepherd had a spine of steel and didn't need him. On paper, Shepherd was perfect. But Raff's heart also belonged to Dante.

Raff didn't know how to love one person and give his soul to another. There was no option that was fair to anyone. As his fated mate, Raff could never claim Shepherd and then disrespect him with Dante. As the love of his life, Raff could never set Dante aside for someone else.

Another wave of panic washed over him. He didn't know what was wrong, but something was just off. It was possible the knowledge alone that Shepherd didn't intend to return was enough to unbalance him. He wouldn't know. Obviously, Raff had never had a mate. Would he feel this way forever if Shepherd stayed gone?

The door to the bar flew open. Dante's emerald gaze swept the room. Raff went on high alert as Dante closed the distance between them. "He's gone."

Raff nodded. "I know. Shepherd stopped by on his way out of town to tell me he was leaving."

"And you let him go?" Dante roared. "Was he alone?"

Raff blinked. He was unaccustomed to Dante's fury, but that was all he got anymore. "Yes, I let him go. He's an adult. I'm not his prison guard. No, he wasn't alone." Even Raff heard the growl to his voice at the admission.

"Who was he with? Did you see him?"

Raff shrugged. "No. He got in an outrageously expensive car and left."

Dante spent a moment visibly trying to kill Raff with his stare. "You are the biggest goddamn dumbass I've ever met in my life and I've lived a long fucking time." Dante growled every word, sounding on the verge of murder. "He left with the demon, you stupid motherfucker. I can't fucking believe you. He's probably already dead, or wishing he was."

There was no air. Raff had been so busy trying to let everything work itself out and trying to pretend he wasn't eaten alive with jealousy that he hadn't once considered his off feeling might be that Shepherd was in trouble. Dante walked away before Raff's mind caught up. He went after him.

"Wait. What the fuck is going on? You never said anything about a demon. You just said he was trying to make a deal to help us. I thought you meant with Jonathan. After all, that's where he went. If you knew a demon had his scent, you should've fucking said something."

Dante spun and went nose to nose with Raff. His fury could be felt like a tangible thing. "I came to your house specifically to tell you about the demon, and you didn't fucking care, Raff. Don't put this on me. Shepherd isn't my mate. He's yours. Yet I was the one trying to keep him safe while you covered your eyes and pretended this wasn't happening. If Shepherd knew a human with an expensive car, why in the hell would he have stayed here?" he screamed, pointing at the ground. "It sure as hell wasn't for your dick, since you've damned well made sure he knew he wasn't wanted, so why, Raff?"

There wasn't a soul in the entire building that wasn't hanging on to their every word. Raff snarled and cast a hard look at the room. "Mind your goddamn business."

Still, no one moved. A direct order from their alpha should've sent the room scurrying, but everyone was obviously invested.

Dante moved even closer, refusing to back down. "Why should they, Raff? This is your pack. Shepherd is your mate. What happens to him happens to them and you've done nothing but embarrass him by refusing to claim him. It's your duty to keep him safe above all others. Yet you've shoved him aside. Tell them why they should listen," Dante demanded. "If you won't protect Shepherd, how are they supposed to trust that you'll protect them? You can stay here and forget him. That's fine. You've proven your point. But I'm going to find Shepherd, or whatever is left of him, and I'll do my best to put him back together. Don't bother to come sniffing around either of us again. You've proven yourself unworthy."

Before Raff could do anything to stop him, Dante dissipated. A very wolf-like growl rent the air. His anger and fear over Shepherd's whereabouts combined to make a volatile mix. He turned, ready to take charge. A room full of eyes stared back at him. He searched out someone he trusted to be quick. His gaze landed on the red-haired girl who worked the bar three nights a week. "Ashka, find Shepherd's brother and send him to Jonathan. He might have some thoughts about where Shepherd would go." He headed for the door, intent on jumping on his motorcycle. Jonathan appeared before he made it three steps. The king's eyes swirled. His anger and worry were tangible. Everyone made a wide berth while several bowed. Most wolves never encountered someone as powerful as Jonathan. Raff had never been happier to see him.

"Jonathan." In one word, Raff's hurt showed itself.

"Let's go," Jonathan said, reaching for him. The room disappeared. The king's home came into view. The living room was filled with familiar faces. He didn't have time to catalog each one. Everyone wore similar concerned stares. Dante wouldn't even look his way.

He didn't get a chance to mull it over. "Tell me what you feel," Jonathan demanded.

Raff was too scared to think straight. "How do you mean?"

Jonathan looked ready to explode. "Concentrate on Shepherd and tell me how you feel."

Raff closed his eyes and took a breath. He focused on his other half. All he felt was the same empty void he'd been experiencing all day. Raff growled in his frustration. "Nothing. It's just like there's a hole where he should be."

Jonathan sat. "That's what I was afraid you'd say."

Panic left Raff with nothing but a ramble of questions. "What do you mean that's what you were afraid of? Is he dead? Are you telling me he's dead? Because I can't hear that, Jonathan." He couldn't. Raff couldn't live with that outcome.

"If Shepherd was dead, I would know. Celeste would tell me, but I can't see him. There's only one place I can't see."

Before Raff had time to experience any relief over the knowledge Shepherd was alive, someone gasped. Raff's gaze followed the sound. It was a small blond who was trying to make himself smaller against Riskel's chest.

Jonathan spoke up as if trying to pull attention away from the man. "I'm sorry, Raff. I don't know how to help this time."

Frustration was beginning to bring out his bad side. "I thought you were all-powerful, Jonathan. If it was one of your mates, my pack would come to your aid. In fact, we have."

"It's not that I don't want to help," Jonathan argued. "The only place I can't see is Hell."

Raff stopped breathing. "What? Are you saying my mate is in Hell? You said he isn't dead. How do we get him out? We have to get him out."

One of Jonathan's mates, Niall, leaned over the back of the couch and set his hands on Jonathan's shoulders, taking over. "It's not that simple. Even if we knew how to get there, which we don't, Jonathan couldn't go. He's too powerful. It would put the entire world at risk should he be taken."

"That's fine. Shepherd is mine. Let's find the place and I'll go in after him." There was nothing Raff wouldn't do.

"It's not enough to know where it is; you need a key," Niall argued. "Demons, even those possessing humans, can enter and leave freely. The rest of us need to be let in, and then every badass upper level evil would come running."

Raff wasn't understanding the holdup. "You have two demons right here." He pointed at Lire and Kallus. "One and two. Surely they know how to get there and won't set off any alarms."

Kallus shook his head. "First off, we're traitors to the Underworld crown. We cannot freely enter Hell. Secondly, the entrance moves. The location is something inside each demon. For obvious reasons, we're no longer privy to that information."

"So let's find a demon and beat the location out of him. I'm not above torturing someone."

"I'll go," the tiny blond said, speaking up. Every head turned his way, and the man tried scrambling away again.

"The hell you say," Risk growled.

Raff ignored Risk and tried making himself look meek, hoping not to scare off the blond. "I'm sorry. We haven't met. I'm Raff."

"Tamil," the sweet one said back in a small voice.

"Tamil is my blood mate," Risk said, explaining the man's presence. "You're not sending him into Hell because you've been careless with your mate."

"It's nice to meet you," Raff said, keeping his gaze locked on Tamil and continuing to ignore Risk.

This was too important to fuck up by losing his temper. "If you think you can get in, I'll be forever grateful. I can't leave my mate there."

Tamil twisted a poppet between his hands, looking a mess of fear and nerves. "If it was Risk in danger, I'd hope you would help me. If I go, it won't set off any alarms."

Risk rubbed Tamil's back. "Baby, you can't do this. I can't watch you do this."

Tamil moved into Risk's hold, as if seeking sanctuary. He was so visibly close to losing his shit, Raff felt hope slip away. Finally, Tamil's gaze moved to Risk and stayed. Raff felt the panic bleed from the man as he stared at his mate as if Risk leached it from him. "I'm the only one who can do this. If it were you, I'd do anything." He swallowed.

Pain stabbed Raff in the chest at the sight of his fear. Risk was right. This child could not do this.

Dante stepped in. "Just tell me where. I'll go in alone. Raff has a pack depending on him, and everyone else here has a mate who needs them. No one will miss me if I don't make it back."

Raff wanted to scream that he would. He would miss Dante every day for the rest of eternity, but he no longer had that right.

Tamil ignored everyone. Never once looking

away from his mate, he cupped Risk's face and held the man's stare. "I love you. Without you, I'm nothing. I can't leave someone to suffer the way I did."

Risk's eyes fell closed, and he pressed his forehead to Tamil's. "I love you, sweets. You can't ask this of me."

Lire stepped forward. "I'll go with Tam. My life is his. No harm will come to your mate in my care."

The pain etched in Risk's features was killing Raff. He swore in that moment he would claim Shepherd the moment he got him back. He would do whatever Goddess Celeste expected of him. Raff recognized his mistakes and would pay any penance. He'd never meant for anyone to get hurt or risk their lives all because he'd wanted Shepherd to want to be with him.

Risk pressed a hard kiss to Tamil's lips. "You come back to me," he growled. "In and out. Understood?"

Tamil nodded. With one last lingering look for his mate, Tamil held a hand out to Lire. As Raff looked on, Lire linked fingers with Tamil before casting a glance his mates' way. He tapped his chest. Faolan and Dougal nodded at whatever silent conversation passed between them. Raff couldn't look away from Tamil's and Lire's joined hands. Tamil held a demon's hand with no visible repercussions. That wasn't possible, but he was seeing it. As Raff looked on, Tamil moved to an antique-looking mirror that hung nearby. He touched the glass. It shimmered—like a silver pond. Tamil looked Risk's way and held the man's stare as he stepped through the mirror, pulling Lire along with him.

Raff's nerves took hold, using his tongue against him. "The entrance to Hell is in your house."

No one spoke.

Raff tore his gaze away from the mirror that was completely normal now. Jonathan stared at him as if waiting for Raff's attention. "The door to Hell is wherever Tamil wants it to be. As a shapeshifter, he takes many forms, including the key to Hell." Raff floundered. He didn't know how to react. Before he found his words, Jonathan continued. "I hope you understand, whenever this over, I'll have to wipe that knowledge from you or you'll never be safe. Tamil will never be safe. I can't allow that."

Raff went back to staring at the mirror. "Once my mate is back under my protection, you can do whatever you want to me. I don't care about anything else right now." The mirror shimmered again, and

Raff went on high alert. His heart jumped into his throat as Tamil reappeared followed closely by Lire. There was no sign of Shepherd. Raff couldn't breathe.

Tamil looked pinched and ready to break. "He's not there."

"You're sure?" Raff barked, hearing the desperation in his voice and incapable of stopping it.

Tamil kept his head down, but Raff saw him nod. He walked into Risk's open arms and collapsed. The pair dissipated before he could demand answers.

Lire's odd mismatched eyes focused on Raff, as if trying to keep him calm. "Your man isn't there. If he was, Tamil would've found him immediately."

"Where did Tamil go? What did he see?"

Lire held his hand up. "Leave the boy be. You have no idea the price he paid for you tonight, but I hope when you find Shepherd, you stop being an idiot. If you understood what you just put Tamil through, you'd never be able to live with the shame."

Raff dragged his fingers through his hair, ready to scream. They all could lecture him later. Right now, he needed answers. "I'll find a way to repay my debt. For now, I need to find my mate. I need help."

Lire looked toward his mates. He chewed his lip, toying with his piercing. No one said a word, as if everyone was equally stumped. With every passing second, Raff's desperation grew. Lire's gaze moved between his mates and Jonathan and back again. "I have a thought." He moved for Faolan. Once he took the amethyst-eyed man's hand, he headed for the door. "Give us five minutes, Jonathan, and then search Faolan out with your mind. I have an idea of how this demon might have Shepherd hidden. Let's test my theory."

Jonathan nodded. "Go. I'm timing you."

The pair disappeared, and Raff paced. Several times, he looked Dante's way, but the vampire kept his head down, as if staring at his shoes or praying. Even Raff didn't know why he looked to Dante. Maybe he sought comfort, or perhaps he sought absolution. Either way, he found neither.

"I can't see Faol," Jonathan said, bringing Raff's focus his way. "There's no void where he should be or anything. He's just gone. What do you feel, Dougal? He's your mate. Can you feel him?"

A line appeared between Dougal's eyes. A smile touched his lips. "Nay, but I know where he is."

Faolan reappeared, smiling. "That's how the bastard is doing it."

Raff looked around the room. He hated being in

the dark while they discussed something that directly affected his mate. "What am I missing?"

Smoke surrounded Faolan, separating from his body before solidifying into Lire. He looked triumphant. "Your mate isn't dead, Raff. He's possessed. Jonathan can't see him because he's not Shepherd right now. He's the demon."

It hit Raff. "He smelled different. When he came to tell me he was leaving, he didn't smell like him. I thought it was odd because I hadn't sensed him coming before he stepped through the door. Holy shit. He was possessed when I saw him earlier."

While Raff tried wrapping his mind around the news, Dante stepped in. "Does that information help you, Jonathan? Can you find specific demons?"

Jonathan nodded and shrugged at the same time. "As long as he's not in Hell, I can find him, but I need to know who I'm looking for. There are a lot of demons roaming the earth."

A growl sounded from Dante. "I don't know how to fix this. This whole damn thing has me fucking helpless. If I'd stayed with him after taking him to Risk's, none of this would've happened. Now I don't know where to start, but I can't stand around and do nothing."

Jonathan stood and circled the couch. He looked

tired. Raff wondered if this was his day every day, dealing with one emergency after the other. Cin and Niall pressed Jonathan between them, as if lending him strength. Jonathan's wings expanded as he wrapped an arm around each man's waist, as if he took a deep breath to soak up their comfort.

With his head bowed, Jonathan spoke to Dante. "You saw the demon, right?"

"Yes. Briefly. I'm not even sure I could describe him. I was too panicked."

Jonathan nodded. "If you want to help, take a walk. Clear your head. It's possible, once you're steadier, you'll remember something important or I'll see your thoughts clearer. All we can do is try."

Dante tilted his chin to the ceiling and took a deep breath before heading for the French doors that led to the backyard. Raff ate Dante alive with his gaze as he walked away. At his darkest moment, he wanted to hold the man who'd held his heart for half a century. He hated himself in that moment because he didn't know how to be the person he needed to be. He didn't know how to let Dante go and be with someone new, but he would. If Goddess Celeste would grant him release from this hell and bring Shepherd home safe, Raff would set Dante free for good.

DANTE SUCKED the night air into his lungs. For Shepherd's sake, he needed to find a place of peace inside his head. It was hard with Raff there. Dante had lived long enough he understood things would change. That was the only certainty in life. No matter the outcome of all this, one day it would be a blurry memory. But right now, he couldn't see past the emotions caving in on him.

The wind whipped through his hair. It carried low voices. Dante turned his head and searched the grounds with his gaze. The long, billowing branches of a willow tree in the distance shifted just right, revealing the couple hiding beneath the tree. His perfect night vision allowed him to see more than he should. Risk and Tamil held each other. Whispered words of love and comfort passed between them. Dante dropped to the ground, sitting to stare like the worst of voyeurs. Tamil was a mystery to Dante. He'd walked into Hell, holding the hand of a demon, and walked out unscathed. While Dante had so many questions, he felt zero desire to ask a single one. The man's secrets were his own. Everyone had them and everyone had the right to keep them. Still, Dante couldn't find the strength to look away from the couple beneath the tree. He'd once had what they did, but then again, he hadn't. He'd found love but not his mate. Perhaps it wasn't the same. Sometimes, it seemed he'd never know. After all, he'd lived half a millennia and never found that piece of his soul. For the past fifty years, that hadn't mattered. He'd been content. Now there was nothing but years and years of solitary existence ahead of him. The idea of it exhausted him.

A large black wolf appeared from the shadows and plopped down beside him. Dante ran his fingers through Evan's fur. He'd always had a soft spot for the boy. Evan was untainted innocence in a world filled with sin. Something about him always filled Dante with hope. He needed that now.

Evan transformed into a man. His gaze stayed locked on the same spot as Dante. "They're beautiful, aren't they? They spend a lot of time out here and I'm always staring."

Dante nodded. "The sight of them together is refreshing when everything else looks so bleak. I know I shouldn't spy on them, but I can't stop."

Evan took his hand and held it. "Sometimes you have to take your comfort where you can."

Dante sucked in a breath, trying to inhale the peace of Evan's presence.

Evan kept talking as if he recognized it was what Dante needed. "Saber and Landry are here. Landry is showing a tiger's mate level of rage over Raff losing his brother. I'm pretty sure, if this wasn't the king's home, Landry would've ripped his throat out by now. Who do you think would win in that fight? I mean, Raff is old and an alpha, but tigers are strong and quick. It's possible Saber would step in and just be like—no one fucks with my mate and ka-bow," Evan said, swiping his arm through the air in a lightning-fast motion. "And tear his heart out. Not that I'd want to see that happen. Just speculating."

Dante's throat swelled. Guilt weighed heavily on his shoulders. "They shouldn't be angry with Raff. Raff didn't lose Shepherd. I did. When I took him to Risk's, I wanted to stay, but it hurt too much to be near him. I left him there alone, knowing he was hurting too. It's my fault."

Evan transformed from overexcited to serious in an instant. "No. No one lost Shepherd. Someone found him and understood his pain at just the right time. Maybe that someone is a no-count demon, or maybe he isn't. The thing is, we don't know. Look at Lire and Kallus. They're both amazing and not necessarily the exception. A lot of demons are just trying to live the lives handed to them. So don't let your head go to the worst place." Evan shook his head as he held Dante's stare. "I can't imagine how Shepherd must feel. Not only did he just find out that everything he believed to be true isn't, he's being told to hand his life over to someone he doesn't know all that well. I wouldn't like finding out that I suddenly don't belong to myself anymore. That all my choices have been stripped away. Someone offered him a chance to decide for himself, while everyone else has been telling him to deal with the life Celeste handed him, and he didn't even know Celeste existed before a few weeks ago." Evan shrugged. "I don't know that I wouldn't have made the same choice in his shoes."

He knew everything Evan said was true. Dante had needed someone to remind him of all those things. He squeezed Evan's hand. "Thank you."

After squeezing him back, Evan released him. "I have to get back to patrol. I just wanted to check on you."

Before Dante could thank him again, Evan turned back into a wolf. Dante didn't watch him leave. A pain bloomed behind his eyes. Dante rubbed his temples. His hair brushed over his shoulder and strong fingers dug into his shoulders and neck. Lips brushed his nape. Dante didn't have the strength to fight anymore tonight. It didn't help that Raff knew exactly how to touch him.

"Do you remember why we worked so well?" Raff asked against his skin. Before Dante could dredge up a passable response, Raff answered his own question. "It's because we always talked to each other. We talked about everything all the time. Nothing was off-limits between us. We openly discussed everything without anger or judgment. That all ended the day Shepherd marked me. You just walked away. I don't understand that because you can still talk to me."

Dante knew it was true. The moment Shepherd marked Raff's skin, Dante had erected a wall between them. It had to stay there for sanity's sake. "There's nothing to say." That wasn't true. There was too much to say. Dante broke. "I wanted more time." The confession fell before Dante could call it back. "We knew this day was coming, but I wasn't ready. I'll never feel like I had enough time with you and it's killing me. Nothing I'm feeling changes anything. You're no longer mine, and you never will be again." Dante met the amber gaze he loved more than life. "I'm still figuring out how to deal with that. You have to help me let you go by letting me go."

Raff opened his mouth. Before any sound fell

from his lips, Raff went still. His nose hit the air. He scanned the grounds with his gaze. "Something's happened."

Dante came to his feet as Raff did. A black wolf alongside a silver wolf burst from the tree line, racing toward the house. Evan and Bleidd didn't slow as they passed. Dante and Raff followed in their tracks. A half step before hitting the door, the pair transformed, becoming men.

"What's wrong?" Dante asked, hearing the panic in his voice.

Evan waved for them to follow. "Bleidd knows who we're dealing with. Come on."

Raff picked up his step, proving his concern for his mate trumped everything, as it should. Dante hated that it still hurt.

When they burst into the living room, everyone turned their way. Jonathan came to his feet. His features were tight with concern. Dante's mind latched on to the fact that Saber and Landry were missing. "What happened to Landry? Shouldn't he be here for this?"

"They went to search places Shepherd might go," Jonathan answered absently. His stare was for Evan alone. "Tell me."

Evan practically bounced in place in his

excitement. "We were at the edge of the property, dealing with that odd deer shifter who keeps coming too close to the alarms, setting them off. Anyhow, Bleidd caught Shepherd's scent as well as a hint of something else." He beamed up at his mate—like he'd never been prouder of anyone. "You know Bleidd has been around since the beginning of time, so he knows all the ancients. It's Stryph."

The round of cursing that tore through the room didn't fill Dante with confidence. "Is he considered an evil demon?" That was honestly all Dante cared about. He couldn't picture Shepherd in the hands of someone harming him. No matter the personal cost, Shepherd was a good man. A kind man. He deserved to be treated as such.

As one of the oldest beings in the room and a god, everyone looked to Eirik for answers. Evan's twin, in every way but blood, scrubbed his hand across his forehead, as if unsure where to start. "He isn't a demon at all."

"Then what is he?" Raff asked, sounding every bit as desperate and confused as Dante felt.

"He's strife," Eirik said, clearing up nothing. "Like, literally," Eirik added. "When Satan was cast down, the heavens shook, and one-third of the angels fell. Everyone knows that, but what most people don't realize is that several of the gods' weapons were cast down to live among the humans as well. We're talking about beings who were here long before there was a here. Stryph is older than the planet you're standing on. In itself, strife isn't necessarily a bad thing. It can bring about healthy competition and crusades that can change the course of history in a positive way. The problem is, Stryph is capable of altering reality until no one can tell what's real. He could be anywhere, and he could've been right here among us for a lot longer than we realize. Who knows what we've experienced lately that was influenced by his interference."

"I don't understand," Raff said, continuing to voice Dante's every thought. "If he didn't come to deal, and he doesn't need to possess Shepherd, what's his end game? Why take Shepherd at all?"

Eirik shrugged. "I can only speculate as to his purpose. It could be exactly what you're seeing. All of us are standing here, looking in one direction, while anything else could be happening in another. I mean, look how many of us are here, trying desperately to find one person while doing things that keep us trapped by our emotions. Tamil made a trip to Hell, the place that mentally damages him the most." Eirik motioned Dante and Raff's way. "A couple who've been together for years has been destroyed. A mate is missing. Jonathan is torn in a thousand directions to the point of weariness. It's just general mayhem and discord around here. Meanwhile, anything could be happening elsewhere. Demons could be plotting an uprising. Fairies might have already taken New York, or whatever crazy thing they do with their time these days. We wouldn't know because we've been here, staring at this."

"I'm sorry," Dante said, speaking up. "I hate to keep revisiting the same points, but what *is* he?"

"An instrument of power," Bleidd said, answering for Eirik, as if he thought he might do a better job of explaining. "But like all weapons, he's neither good nor bad, merely a tool that can be used for either. He doesn't answer to the heavens or the underworld. Stryph serves no purpose but his own. He just keeps life in balance by any means necessary. Stryph can't be reined in or destroyed. Every being, mortal and immortal, lives at the mercy of his whims. It seems, currently, Shepherd serves his motives. Whatever they may be."

"The hell you say," Raff barked, sounding enraged. His blazing gaze stayed locked on Jonathan.

"Now that you know who you're dealing with, can you find him? I'll go after the bastard."

A line appeared between Jonathan's brows. His chest expanded. It was as if he turned inward, searching. His face went pale. A gasp tore from Niall's throat and he shot to his feet in just enough time to catch Jonathan as he collapsed. All Dante could do was watch in horror as the room exploded into action, doing everything possible to save an obviously fading Jonathan. The gravity of the situation fell on Dante, suffocating him. Without Jonathan, all hope was lost.

FOUR

THE HOUSE WAS QUIET. SHEPHERD STARED AT the unfamiliar ceiling for several minutes before allowing his mind to accept the reality of his situation. He was in Stryph's bed but obviously no longer possessed. Everything was dark except the thin line of light that peeked around the window's blackout curtains. He didn't have the slightest clue of the time or even the day. Everything had slipped away from him with Stryph in charge.

After sitting up, Shepherd let his feet drop to the floor. For a moment, he gathered his bearings and eyed his body. Soft pajama pants covered the lower half of his body, while his chest remained bare. Considering the flashes he'd caught of his night with Stryph manning the controls of his body, Shepherd expected to be hungover, exhausted, and sore. Instead, he felt refreshed. His mind was clear. He pushed to his feet and followed his nose down the stairs. The smell of coffee permeated the air. Shepherd slowed as the kitchen came into view. Dark wood, even darker granite, and black appliances would've made most kitchens seem small. Stryph's was large enough to handle the color scheme and the giant island in the center without feeling crowded. His socked feet padded across the hardwood floor without making a sound. He was grateful for the chance to watch Stryph without being noticed.

Stryph looked amazing standing in the kitchen shirtless while pouring his coffee. His body was sleek, and he moved like a predator. It seemed Shepherd had a thing for animalistic men. Having someone in his head was obviously another thing he found appealing. The more someone shoved their way in, the happier he was—like he was tired of being in charge. Shepherd didn't think he was very good at handling life by himself. After all, he'd been fucking it up as long as he could recall. Maybe he just needed to let someone else take the reins.

"Would you like something to eat?"

Shepherd smiled at getting caught. He automatically moved closer. "Don't you sleep?"

Stryph turned and met his stare. Shepherd was blown away anew by the man's odd-colored eyes. "Would you like me to?"

He felt his brows pull together in confusion. "Why does it matter what I want? Either you need sleep to survive or you don't, right?"

Stryph turned and leaned against the counter with his cup held between his hands. "If you'd like for me to crawl into bed beside you and sleep, I will. Otherwise, no, I don't need sleep to survive. Surviving implies I'm a living creature. In truth, I'm more of an endless energy source, existing where I please. Since it currently pleases me to please you, would you like me to sleep?"

Rather than answer and give away any of himself, Shepherd chose to latch on to another part of his statement. "Are you telling me that an endless energy source needs coffee? If so, what hope is there for the rest of us?"

The way Stryph's mouth twitched with barely suppressed humor did something odd to Shepherd's chest. "Haven't you ever heard that coffee is the elixir of the gods?"

A chuckle fell from Shepherd's lips before he

could stop it. His feet moved him closer to Stryph without his permission. "Yesterday, you were a demon and then royalty. Today, you're a god. What will you be this afternoon?" He thought it over for a second. "What's more powerful than a god?"

"You'd be surprised," Stryph said, openly smiling this time. He shook his head as if he didn't know what to think. "You baffle me, Mr. LaTour. Why does someone so filled with love care so little about themselves? It's counterintuitive—like taking a southern route to a northern destination. But that brings me to another topic," he said, not giving Shepherd time to answer. "There's still the matter of keeping my end of our deal. Well," Stryph said, motioning carelessly. "Actually, I already have. If you leave here now, you can head straight to Raff and you'll know what to do when you get there. If you're honest with yourself, you've always known what to do." Shepherd couldn't deny it. He knew there was only way to make things right. Stryph sipped his coffee before setting it aside and focusing on Shepherd once more. "Or I could offer you an alternative."

"I'm listening." Shepherd would be lying if he said he wasn't curious.

Stryph crossed the room and closed the distance

between them. Shepherd's back hit the fridge as Stryph stole every inch of space between them. "You could choose me."

Shepherd's hands lifted without thought. His palms slid across Stryph's hips. He drew the man closer.

"How do you mean?"

"Stay," Stryph said, making it sound so easy. "I'll keep you spoiled. You'll never want for anything or wonder about your worth. We could have so much fun together. Imagine the trouble we could start."

Besides the stabbing pains in his chest over the idea of never seeing Raff or Dante again, Shepherd knew nothing was ever simple or free. "What do you hope to gain in exchange for this picture-perfect life you're painting?"

"You. A partner in crime." Before Shepherd had time to absorb that detail, Stryph glanced over his shoulder, as if seeing something Shepherd didn't. "I'm sorry, but you'll have to make your decision quickly. Your mate is losing his patience. They'll come for you soon."

Shepherd's mind froze. He didn't know how to feel. Nothing made sense any longer. All he'd wanted was to make his own choices. To choose who he wanted without anyone's insight. Now everything was rushed again, and he was just... lost.

Stryph massaged his arms. His light gaze never wavered. A sad smile touched his lips. "It's okay, sexy. I know you're tired. I'll fix your life." Everything went hazy as Stryph leaned in and touched his lips to Shepherd's, and then everything was gone.

RAFF PACED THE HALLWAY. He couldn't stop. Nothing felt right or good. Jonathan was locked behind his bedroom door, being treated by his mates. Dante had disappeared hours ago, and Shepherd was still out there somewhere in Goddess Celeste only knew what condition. Their lives had been upended, and no one knew why. Possibly they were being kept distracted from something even worse that was already on its way. Maybe they were being tested. The whys didn't matter to Raff. He wanted... Raff massaged his chest, trying to answer that question or possibly holding in the truth. He stopped and stared out the window at the pounding rain that bounced from the leaves of a nearby tree. Raff wanted to tear apart the world until he found his mate. Then he wanted to lock Shepherd away, claim him, and never look away. It was a slap in the face to the life he'd lived for the past fifty years, but he couldn't change the way he felt. When he'd met Dante all those years ago, his mate hadn't been born yet. The other half of his soul had been with Celeste, waiting for a new body to inhabit. Now they were supposed to be together and Raff had squandered his chance. Even worse, now there was part of his soul out there at the mercy of a being that could do anything without conscience.

Something moved at the corner of his vision, dragging Raff's attention away from the window. Evan and Tamil lingered at the mouth of the hallway. They faced each other, hands moving but not lips, as if they were having a silent argument. Tamil noticed him watching and scrambled out of sight. Evan followed at a slower pace. They were an odd pair. Raff went back to staring out the window. Maybe if he focused hard enough, he could call out to Shepherd, even though they weren't officially mated. Another tiny movement dragged Raff's attention back toward the end of the hall. Tamil and Evan were back. This time, it was doubly obvious they spoke mentally. The idea caught and held his attention. They weren't mates. That shouldn't be possible.

"How do you hear each other's thoughts?"

Two sets of eyes shot his way. They froze as if he'd busted them doing something illegal. Neither man looked at him directly. They visibly searched for a lie. Tamil broke first. "Bleidd touched me once and since I'm—" Evan slapped a hand over Tamil's mouth, cutting off his words.

"Annual orgy incident gone awry," Evan yelled, sounding panicked as he dragged Tamil out of sight. He could hear their rapid whispering around the corner but couldn't make out their words.

With a shake of his head, Raff went back to pacing. His gaze kept sliding back toward the mouth of the hall. Evan and Tamil kept popping into sight and back out again, wrestling like children. Raff rolled his eyes. Pups. It blew him away that Evan had been chosen by Odin to be the guardian wolf of a god's mate. The boy was... well, a boy. Not only had he snagged a coveted role in the wolf chain of command, he'd been fated an ancient alpha mate. It was mind boggling. Yet, it wasn't. Raff genuinely liked Evan. He was pure of heart and would die for his people. Holding on to those things through everything life threw someone's way, that was a true test of character. Raff had failed at life long ago.

Tamil flew around the corner, heading his way. Evan was right behind him. "No, Tam. Risk still hasn't recovered from what you did last night. He'll be so upset. I don't want another to the grave secret. One exploding demon in a lifetime is enough."

Exploding demon. What the hell?

Tamil froze and focused on Evan. "Just like with the demon chunks thing, I'll sneak back into bed and Risk will be fine. Plus, once Shepherd is back, everyone will know he's here, so it won't be a secret. Jonathan needs peace to recover. I can give it to everyone." He looked Raff's way and spoke quickly, as if he expected Evan to cover his mouth again. "I can get Shepherd."

Raff's heart jumped into his throat. "What? How?"

Tamil didn't look quite as confident with Raff's intense focus on him. Raff tried making himself less intimidating. Even though it didn't seem to help, Tamil didn't back down. "Last night, you learned something about me, but then Jonathan took the memory from you to keep us both safe. So, I can't tell you exactly why I can get him. But now that I know who has Shepherd, and since Jonathan can't help you right now, I sort of feel like I should go get him."

Raff didn't want to insult Tamil, but he didn't look strong enough to do anything. He cleared his throat, trying to think of a way to say as much without insulting the man. Tamil was beautiful and fragile-looking—like a tiny porcelain doll. No doubt he made the perfect docile mate to comfort Riskel's life, but he was very obviously not a warrior. "Um. Why don't you tell me where he is, and I'll go?"

Evan and Tamil exchanged glances. They looked uncomfortable. This time, Evan was the one clearing his throat. "No offense, but you're not strong enough for this."

A snort escaped Raff before he could call it back. "You're both very sweet. I haven't been the alpha of the southeast pack for over two hundred years for nothing. Just give me an address and I'll handle this."

Tamil cocked his head to one side and eyed Raff like he thought he was insane. "So you think you'll just bust into the home of Stryph, grab Shepherd, and what? Drive away?"

"Well, when you say it all out loud like that..." Raff shook his head. "But ridiculous or not, if you know where he is, I don't want to wait until one of the vamps around here can pop in and out. A million and one horrible things could happen between now and whenever Jonathan is stable or whatever. Add in the fact that it also has to be nighttime for them to dissipate; fuck, it could be forever from now. My nerves can't take the waiting."

Tamil now ran the dress of a doll Raff hadn't noticed him holding before between his fingers. He didn't look like he was really getting what Raff was saying. No one currently unoccupied with the king had the power to do what Tamil planned. A loud sigh rent the air as Tamil handed the doll to Evan. "Don't let anything happen to her," he said, sounding harder than Raff imagined the man could. Before anyone could respond, Tamil was gone. Raff stared at the spot where Tamil had been, unsure of how to react. Something niggled at the back of his mind. He'd learned something mind-blowing about Tamil the night before, but he couldn't recall what. Before Raff had time to work through a single thought, Tamil was back. With his arms locked around Shepherd's chest, he labored under the weight of holding the unconscious man. Raff's first reaction was his most telling. His throat swelled at the sight of his heart in Tamil's arms. He couldn't go back to living without Shepherd.

EVERYTHING WAS DARK, loud, and crushing his brain. Jonathan couldn't focus, breathe, or open his eyes. Too many people were silently screaming in their heads and praying he could make it stop. Meanwhile, he was paralyzed, incapable of helping a single soul, even those closest to him.

Warm lips brushed his nape. Another set settled against the corner of his mouth and lingered. The combined scent of his mates overcame him. Everything fell silent inside his mind. The pain slowly lessened. He inhaled deeper, inflating his lungs with their essence.

"That's it, sexy. Breathe."

Cin's voice sounded like it came from a distance, even though he could feel his touch.

Niall's hand massaged his hip. "You can't scare us like this."

He always knew the difference between their hands and lips, even with his eyes closed. They were unique in their own ways, yet they equally held Jonathan's heart. He would never leave them. No matter how hard he fought to say as much, nothing worked. His body was still paralyzed.

"If you leave, I'll follow. I know you don't want that, but I don't want to be here without you."

"Aye," Cin said, joining Niall's insane plan. "I'll go too. Nothing matters to me except the people in this bed."

They were in bed? That was odd. Jonathan had been plotting Shepherd's return only a moment ago, and then... and then... nothing. There was nothing.

"Follow your mates' voices back to us, Jonathan," Lire said, confusing Jonathan further. "What will become of your clan if all its leaders are gone? I could visit you, but Dougal, Faolan, and Riskel wouldn't see you again. Think of how that would destroy poor Evan and Tamil. They can't take the blow."

Panic rose in Jonathan's chest, choking him. Why was everyone talking like he was dead? He was right there, squeezed between his mates.

A knocking came from miles away, barely kissing Jonathan's ears. Shuffling and cursing followed.

"Now is nae the time," Dougal barked. Whispered words followed. Jonathan fought to make them out without luck. A door slammed in the distance, sounding like a hollow echo.

"We're alone now, gorgeous. You can open your eyes. Please," Cin begged. Jonathan's fingers found a loop on his jeans. He managed a small tug. It felt like a victory. Happiness filled Cin's voice. "I felt that little tug. You'll have to work harder than that if you want me out of my jeans. You did nae marry an easy man."

"Liar." The word burst from Jonathan's lips yet sounded weak. "I had you two hours after we met. Niall's the one who made me wait."

Niall's arms encircled him and tightened enough to cut off his air. "But I wanted you before you knew I existed," Niall whispered against his throat, sounding choked.

"I don't know what's wrong with me," Jonathan admitted, hearing the fear in his voice. "I can't get my body to do anything I tell it to do."

"It's okay," Cin said. His voice soothed him. "We've got you. Tam says you focused too hard on a being much stronger than you. Stryph obviously didn't like you pushing at his mind, trying to find him, so he shoved you away. The mental blast took you down."

The memory returned. He'd pushed too hard. The move had been unintentional. He'd just hoped to find Stryph quickly and get Shepherd home. Jonathan had expected Stryph to be hard to track down, and he'd blasted too much energy the man's way. It didn't appear Stryph appreciated the mental intrusion. He didn't care to repeat the experience.

"Note to self, don't piss off Stryph."

"You're growing stronger by the minute. That's what's important."

Jonathan nodded at Niall's observation. "I just need a little longer and I'll find Shepherd."

"No." Niall's harsh tone surprised Jonathan. "You've done enough for everyone else. The world can care for itself for a while. You need a break or it's only a matter of time before you crack. I've ordered everyone to back the fuck off, and I put out the 'closed for complaints' sign. You're off duty, Jonathan."

"Don't worry," Cin said, sounding calmer than Niall, as if he was playing peacemaker. "Tam has Shepherd. There's nothing immediate that needs to be done. No more playing the fireman for you. For our sakes, just stay put."

"Is Shepherd okay?" Jonathan felt his blood pressure rise. The need to check on everyone was already overwhelming him despite not being able to open his eyes.

Cin sounded hurt when he spoke again. "When do we get to come first?"

Guilt crashed down on Jonathan, crushing him.

He forced himself to let everything else go. "You two are always first with me."

"Then prove it, goddamn it," Niall snapped. "Let everyone else sort out their shit without you for once. You do a lot of good. No one is denying that, but you won't be any use to anyone dead, especially us. If you love us at all, stay put for a few days. Let us baby you. It'll take us a minute to get over the ever-living fuck you just scared out of us."

Jonathan relaxed deeper into Niall's hold. A happy sigh escaped him as his mate's warmth engulfed him. He managed to pry one eye open. Cin stared back at him. His features were pinched, and he chewed on his bottom lip.

"Goddamn, it's not fair for one person to be so sexy."

Cin's expression cleared and a lecherous grin pulled at his lips. "Don't compliment me. I only made it two hours after we met. Nowadays, I'm even less patient. I'd hate to take advantage of you in your weakened state."

Jonathan snaked his hand between Niall's body and his. He cupped the man's package as he openly taunted Cin. "I thought you wanted to keep me in bed."

"To rest, minx," Niall said as he kissed the shell

of Jonathan's ear. It was too late. He'd heard the hint of laughter in Niall's voice. Half the battle was already won.

"Well, I mean, there's two of you and only one of me. I don't see why I always have to do all the work."

Niall pinched his ass—hard. "You're a little shit starter."

Cin nodded. "Don't think we don't see right through your ploy."

Jonathan released a long, weary-sounding sigh. "Rejected again."

"Are you kidding me?" Niall's voice was heavy with laughter, but Jonathan knew he had him.

"We've never rejected you. Not once," Cin said, sounding insulted.

Jonathan rolled onto his back, crossed his arms over his chest, and stared at the ceiling. Cool air brushed over his skin, making him realize he was nude. "It's okay. I'm sure my pride will recover. One day, someone will come along who wants me." Jonathan sniffed loudly. "They won't strip me in my sleep and then reject me."

"You lost your kilt when you shrank back to bite-sized Jonathan while unconscious."

"Yeah," Cin said, having Niall's back. "Maybe we enjoyed it a little and unanimously decided not to cover your incredibly sexy body, but we didn't tease you."

"You ogled my nakedness while I slept," Jonathan said, reaching for his most obnoxious and accusing tone. "You know I can't achieve my best angle while unconscious."

"First off," Niall said, easily snagging Jonathan around the waist and slipping beneath him until Jonathan sprawled across him like a mattress. "Your every angle is an amazing angle." His hand found Jonathan's cock. "Secondly, we've been ogling you in your sleep for years."

Cin shifted to his knees and crawled their way. "Don't worry, baby. We've always made sure you were awake for the good parts." He licked Jonathan's crown.

A gasp escaped Jonathan.

Niall tilted his chin up, forcing Jonathan to meet his gaze. "You ready to get double stuffed?"

The snort escaping Jonathan died on a moan as Niall's tongue filled his mouth. Cin's hot mouth opened over his nipple. Jonathan went into sensory overload as Cin helped Niall undress. He felt stronger by the second. His powers grew. Jonathan knew he could snap his fingers and the pair would be every bit as nude as him. Instead, he relinquished control, resting his powers as his mates requested. Their needs came first, even if what they required was Jonathan being docile.

The moment he found himself stretched wide to the point of painful, their emotions overwhelmed Jonathan. They were scared and sometimes felt shoved aside by the weight of Jonathan's duty. His lungs burned. Tears pricked at the backs of his eyes. These men were everything to him. He'd always known if the choice came down to them or watching the world burn, he'd watch the world burn every time. But they didn't know it and that killed Jonathan.

"I'm sorry," Jonathan choked out, ruining the moment. Cin froze with his fangs sunk into Jonathan's chest. Niall held him tighter, as if trying to squeeze out the pain. Jonathan's breaths came faster by the second. He couldn't stop the flood of emotions. "I never meant to make either of you feel cheated. It crushes me that you're unhappy being mated to me." He couldn't stop the oncoming panic attack. Losing Cin and Niall wasn't an option. He wouldn't survive it. Hurting them was a two-ton weight on his windpipe.

While crushed between them, Niall and Cin

kissed every place they could reach. They shushed him, trying to comfort him.

"Breathe, baby," Cin whispered against his skin.

He tried. His voice sounded winded and strained when he spoke. "I'm trying." He gulped and gasped, fighting for oxygen. "I can work harder. You won't get pushed aside again. I didn't mean to fail either of you. Your unhappiness is choking me. I love you both. Please don't leave me. I can figure out how to give you more."

"Goddamn," Niall cursed, rolling until they were on their sides and the pair could crush him between them. "Stop, Jonathan. No one is going anywhere. The only thing that makes us unhappy is watching you killing yourself. But Cin and I both know we can step in and slow you down at any moment. We know you'll always stop whatever you're doing to be alone with us."

Jonathan's teeth chattered. Niall's words and the cadence of his voice slowly drained away the fear.

"Come here," Niall said, urging Jonathan onto his back. His lips touched Jonathan's. As their tongues met, Niall pulled Cin into their kiss. Love overwhelmed every other emotion filling him. He could feel their affection.

Jonathan buried his fingers in Niall's and Cin's

hair, holding them tight as they pressed their foreheads together. "I don't understand what happened," Jonathan whispered as he felt the last tendrils of panic ebb.

"I have a bad feeling I do." Niall's tone turned dark. "I don't think it's Shepherd they just rescued, or at least, I don't think he came back alone."

"Naturally," Cin said, summing up Jonathan's thoughts perfectly. It wouldn't be their lives if something went right. Now they had Stryph under their roof, and—fuck all—Jonathan was exhausted.

FIVE

Considering all the things they'd done over the years, Jonathan didn't think he had it in him to still blush. Each time he thought about the ways Niall and Cin had taken care of him, while he did nothing except enjoy their touch, Jonathan's face heated. While Cin had disappeared an hour earlier to ensure the perimeter was patrolled for the day and everyone ate like they should, Niall had stuck around. They'd taken a hot bath together before Niall carried him to bed, tucking him beneath the covers. His eyes should've been heavy, but Jonathan didn't really need sleep any longer. Instead, he floated on a cloud of euphoria. Even though he could still feel the heaviness of Stryph's presence, his mates had cleared his mind.

Niall's lips brushed over his. "Rest, angel. You are the greatest love of my life. I'll check on Shepherd."

"I love you so much," Jonathan whispered as he stole another quick kiss. He missed having days where responsibilities didn't drag them in opposite directions. But it mattered to him that everyone else in the house was happy too, so he let Niall go. On his way out, as the bedroom door swung open, Jonathan caught sight of Tamil sitting on the floor in Risk's lap in the hallway. Tamil's chin shot up and his worried gaze peered around Niall's large frame.

From his spot on the bed, Jonathan gave Tamil a tiny finger wave. "What's up, sweetie?"

"Tam's been worried," Risk said, explaining why they were camped out right outside Jonathan's bedroom door.

Jonathan lifted the covers and gave the mattress a pat, inviting them to join him.

Tam sneaked a peek Niall's way, as if he expected to get turned away.

"Go on," Niall said, waving them into the room. "As long as Jonathan stays in bed, you're good to hang out with him. If someone doesn't keep him company, he's likely to try to sneak in some work." He wasn't wrong.

The pair stood and made their way inside the room. While Risk chose the reading chair near the bed, Tamil climbed in next to Jonathan. He sat cross-legged and twisted the tail of his shirt, looking ready to break.

"Are you okay?"

Jonathan nodded. "Cin says Baptiste is on his way over to ward the room against all outside influences. As long as I stay here and get some rest, I should be clear of all Stryph's influence soon."

"I wonder why he affects you more than anyone else."

Jonathan shrugged. "My guess is that I'm just weakened at the moment. I think—once I'm back on my feet—he won't have such a negative impact on me. For now, I promised Cin and Niall I would rest. As hard as it is for me to do nothing, I intend to keep my word."

"Do you need us to do anything?" Risk asked.

His question made Tamil bounce a little. "Oh, do you want me to try to heal you? I mean, I'm not strong like you, but it might help a little."

Jonathan took Tamil's hand. He stroked him with his thumb because he genuinely loved Tamil and wished he could make Tamil see how beautiful he was inside. Jonathan held Tamil's stare, hoping the man would see the truth in his eyes. "Tam, you are the strongest person I know. I can't hold a candle to your abilities." Tam opened his mouth, as if to argue. Jonathan shook his head. "It's true. One of these days, you'll leave me behind, and when you look back at the time you were here, you won't recognize yourself. I hope when that day comes, you won't forget about me. You're one of my favorite people. I love you a lot, you know."

Tamil stared at his lap. As Jonathan looked on, a tear rolled down Tamil's cheek. He swiped it away. When he spoke, his voice came out sounding small. "I love you a lot too, but I don't know if I'll ever be strong enough to leave here. You have no idea how much I feel like I'm failing because I know Risk misses his home." He swiped at his face again. "But I'm scared of being in a huge house where I'll be alone sometimes. Plus, it sort of reminds me of a time I don't want to remember. I know I need to face it and be a better mate." He sniffed. The sound hurt Jonathan's heart. "I'm just failing."

Risk moved to join them on the bed. He wrapped his arm around Tamil's other side. "Sweets, nothing matters to me as much as you do. You couldn't fail me if you tried. I don't care if we stay here for good, as long as Jonathan doesn't get sick of us. If I have you, I don't need anything else."

"I shouldn't be dumping on you," Tam said, sounding even more upset. "You're supposed to be resting."

"I am," Jonathan said with a chuckle. "With the way there's always one emergency right after the other around here, I feel like I don't get enough of this—time alone with the people I'm closest to." It occurred to him he hadn't addressed Risk's words. "Oh, and it's not possible for me to get sick of you. This is a family here. Stay as long as you want. If that means forever, then I'm fine with that. In fact, I'd be ecstatic. I love having both of you here. It has the added bonus of bringing Evan and his crew around too. We're all stronger together."

Tamil flashed him a shy smile before going back to staring at his lap. He squeezed Jonathan's hand. A warmth traveled up Jonathan's arm. Bliss settled over Jonathan as if all his cares had been carried away. "I fixed the damage Stryph caused. You should still stay in bed since you promised, but you shouldn't feel sad anymore."

Jonathan sat up. Without thought, he gave Tam a quick hug and kissed his cheek before settling back down on his side. Tamil's blush made the impulsive move worthwhile. "You're a treasure. Risk won the lotto with you."

"Damn right," Risk growled, sounding possessive and making Jonathan smile.

Tamil's gaze moved over the room, as if trying not to meet anyone's stare. It couldn't be more obvious praise made him uncomfortable. "I think I'll check on Shepherd. He's probably exhausted."

Jonathan's heart rate kicked up. "You shouldn't go near Shepherd. That's not him."

A sweet, light blue stare finally settled on him. Tamil didn't look scared or worried. "It's still Shepherd in control. Don't worry. I can feel Stryph. He's protecting Shepherd. I haven't figured out why yet, but I can feel his determination to keep Shepherd safe."

Jonathan's mind whirled with new information. He hated not knowing what was happening. After taking a deep breath, Jonathan tried letting it go. He'd promised he'd relax and he damn well would. If he wanted Tamil to believe in himself, he needed to let go so Tam could fly. He was still here if anyone needed him. For now, he'd do nothing.

NO MATTER how hard he tried, Raff couldn't tear his gaze from Shepherd's sleeping form. Shepherd was there. He was breathing, but Raff didn't know if he was okay. No matter what they tried, he wouldn't wake. Physically, he seemed fine. There were no marks on his body. Raff had thoroughly checked. It was like Shepherd's shell was there, but his soul was somewhere else.

Raff didn't know how else to cling to his sanity, so he started talking. "I knew you were special the first time I saw you." Raff shook his head as the memory of that night filled his mind. "The pool hall was packed that night. I was tossing beers on the bar faster than I could think. You weren't as loud as everyone else when you ordered, but I heard you in my head louder than any voice I'd ever encountered. When I glanced your way, for the first time in my life, I understood the definition of describing someone as 'stunning.' You stopped me cold." A smile tugged at Raff's lips as he stared at Shepherd. "I couldn't look away as I moved closer. You probably thought I was a crazy person," Raff said with a snort. "I'm pretty sure I didn't blink. My first thought was if this guy isn't a famous model or actor, than life has royally fucked him." Raff's smile fell. "Then we talked for a while and I realized life really had fucked you. I've never wanted to save anyone before. You're the exception." Raff stroked Shepherd's bottom lip with his thumb. His eyes followed the motion. "When you lost your job and apartment, I needed to rescue you. Then I realized you're my mate, and the need to give you a home doubled, but you won't let me. Your pride is so beautiful. I don't want to break it to ensure your needs are met. While I've been trying to figure out how to fit into your life, you've been trying to get away, but you frustrate the hell out of me. I don't know what to do, Shep. You're always angry with me. I can feel your rage banging against my soul all hours of the day. You've made your point. I know you don't want me." His stare moved over Shepherd's rugged and perfect features. "I want you." As the whispered confession fell from his lips, they solidified in his heart. His voice grew stronger. "Since the first moment we met, I've been obsessed with the idea of you. The guilt has been massive. Dante deserved better from me. When he invited you home with us, he gave me just enough rope to hang myself with and I happily jumped to my death. I was all in, making love to you, giving you a job where I had you at my side every day, and bringing you to live under my roof." Raff swallowed past a lump in his throat. His rage grew with every word. "Then you sliced me with that knife and walked away. Fuck you for that, Shepherd. Fuck you for giving exactly what I wanted because now I want you to love me back and you won't. I'm stuck here, wanting to kiss you now, and you won't fucking wake up and kiss me."

"You're spoiled." Before Raff had time to be surprised over Shepherd's words or consciousness, Shepherd hauled Raff in for a kiss. His chest felt ready to burst. Between the fear he wouldn't find Shepherd alive and the belief Shepherd would never touch him again, Raff had been on the verge of breaking down. Shepherd moaned. The backs of Raff's eyes burned. He should pull away and demand answers. Raff couldn't. Shepherd had been the one to initiate their kiss. In his heart, Raff had believed Shepherd would never accept him. Now Shepherd was willingly kissing him, and Raff's gums itched. The need to bite and claim his mate overwhelmed him. Before it became an issue, the door burst open. For a half second, they froze—lips clinging. As one, they looked toward the open doorway. Landry looked every bit as surprised as Raff felt.

"Baby brother," Shepherd said loudly, shaking Raff from his shock.

"Um." Landry scrubbed the back of his neck, looking uncomfortable and visibly trying not to look directly at them. "I came as soon as I heard you'd been found." His shoulders squared. He met Raff's gaze. "Raff, do you mind if I have a minute with my brother?"

Even though Raff didn't want to let Shepherd out of his sight, he slipped from the bed. He met Shepherd's stare. "I'll be right outside the door if you need me."

Shepherd flashed him a smile as he worked his way into a seated position. "Okay. Don't worry. My baby brother is here. I'll be fine."

Raff gave Shepherd one final look. His eyes didn't want to move away, but Shepherd's brother had a right to see him. Once he hit the hallway, he pulled the door closed behind him. He found Saber waiting.

"How is Shep?" Saber asked the instant Raff looked his way.

Raff fought an unexpected blush over the way they'd been caught and his wayward thoughts. Shepherd was damn good, as always. That was why the man had snagged him in the first place. Raff couldn't say that. "He seems fine. I didn't get a lot of time to question him before Landry showed up."

A stirring at the mouth of the hallway pulled Raff's attention away from Saber before the tiger could ask him anymore questions. Niall's long stride ate up the length of the hall as he headed their way. His tightened features sent Raff's heart racing. Raff had been so busy with Shepherd, he hadn't checked on Jonathan.

"Is Jonathan okay?" Raff asked before Niall made it the length of the room.

Niall gave him a sharp nod. "He'll be better once Baptiste finishes warding our bedroom against all outside influences. Where's Shepherd?"

Saber motioned toward the closed bedroom door. "We're giving him a few minutes with Landry."

"I'm not sure that's such a good idea. We have reason to believe he's still possessed by Stryph."

"Stryph," Saber repeated before Raff could respond. "Why would that guy possess anyone?"

Their gazes swung Saber's way. Raff beat Niall to the punch. "You know Stryph?"

"Um, yeah," Saber said, dragging out the final word. "So do you. He's at the pool hall all the time."

"What?" Surely if a being older than time hung out at his bar, Raff would know.

Saber nodded. His expression screamed he thought Raff was daft. "I've shot pool with him countless times. Dozens of times when you've spoken to him with me standing right there spring to mind."

Raff made a helpless gesture. "I don't remember any of this."

"He's that blond guy who looks dead up like a Viking. His head is shaved bald on both sides," Saber said, slicking his hair back on both sides as if that helped paint the picture. "But the center part of his hair is kind of like a mohawk in long braids."

The memory hit Raff. He snapped his fingers. "Oh, he has really light-colored eyes. They're almost eerie to look at."

Saber nodded. "Yep, that's him."

"Goddamn," Raff breathed without thought. "That dude's ridiculously hot, but he's quiet and somewhat mean-looking. He doesn't invite conversation." Raff shook his head. "I can't believe this. How have I been feet from someone so powerful and not known it?"

Niall cut in. "I think you should probably check on your mate, Saber."

A deep line appeared between Saber's brows. "He asked for time alone with his brother. I can feel him. He's fine. Stryph's a good guy. He wouldn't harm my mate. In truth, I can't picture him hurting anyone. But I have to say that was Shepherd I just saw in there."

Raff nodded. "I have to agree. That's Shepherd. I know my mate's scent."

Niall scrubbed his hands through his hair. "Damned if I know what's going on around here. I'm sorry, Raff. Until we know the full story, I have to ask that Shepherd doesn't leave."

"That's fine," Raff said, willing to accept Niall's order for now. "I'd feel safer with more eyes on him, so he doesn't disappear again." He couldn't go through that again. As if the thought alone of losing Shepherd brought on a phantom ache, the center of his chest suddenly hollowed, as if his heart had been ripped from his chest.

Saber's gaze shot to the closed door—like he felt the same disturbance in the air. "Something's wrong." Saber leapt for the door and threw it open. Panic shot through Raff. He followed on Saber's heels, resisting the urge to shove the tiger aside. Landry was alone on the bed, unconscious.

"Fook." Niall's curse behind him summed up Raff's thoughts too.

Saber skidded to a stop at the edge of the bed and cupped Landry's face. The second he touched him, Landry's eyes shot open. Saber's sharp inhalation of relief sounded loud throughout the room. He dropped to his knees and pressed his forehead to Landry's chest. Saber sucked air. "Holy shit," Saber said, sounding shook. "What the hell just happened?"

Landry ran his hand through Saber's hair. "What's wrong, baby? Are you okay?"

Saber sat back on his heels. "You scared me. What happened with Shepherd? Where did he go?"

Landry looked around. His expression screamed confusion. "I don't know. Shepherd told me everything was fine, and he loves me. He said he had everything figured out, and he'd always been proud to call me his baby brother, then nothing. You were here, looking freaked."

"I don't understand. Where the hell did he go? How did he get past us?"

"It's Stryph. He could do any damn thing," Niall said, sounding defeated.

Raff tilted his chin to the ceiling and tried breathing away the massive pain weighing him down. He'd lived a long time. In all his years, he couldn't remember a time when he'd been dealt so much in such a short time. To an outsider, Shepherd's constant disappearances might not seem like a nightmare. For Raff, having a missing and unclaimed mate was like having his body constantly ravaged by sharks. Shepherd had walked away the second he'd learned he was a wolf mate. He hadn't stopped running away since. Raff didn't know how to fix anything. He didn't know any goddamn thing anymore.

DANTE GRABBED the last of his clothes from the dresser and tossed them in a backpack. When he'd left the home he shared with Raff and moved in with the king, he'd let Raff keep everything except his personal things. Since he planned to shift from one place to the next, he needed to travel light. Shepherd was home and safe. It was time for Dante to make his exit.

"What? No goodbye?"

Dante spun, clutching his chest. His heart beat so fast Dante wondered if it would leap from his chest. Shepherd sat on his bed. "Goddamn it, Shep. How the hell did you get in here?"

Shepherd shrugged. "The door wasn't locked. You were pretty damn preoccupied, trying to make a run for it without anyone noticing."

"I'm not running," Dante said, dropping his hand

and the bag he held. "There's just no longer a reason for me to stay. It looks like you walked away from your ordeal unscathed. The time has come for Raff to claim you. No one needs me anymore. The faster I go, the better for everyone."

"Huh," Shepherd said, sounding dry. "That's rich. You must be the blindest bastard on the planet if that's the way you see it." Shepherd's calm expression made it impossible for Dante to as much as blink. It was obvious whatever had gone on with Shepherd during his time with Stryph had been what he needed. Shepherd looked like a man who knew his mind.

Dante cleared his throat. His mouth suddenly felt dry. "Tell me which part I got wrong."

"Almost everything you said is bullshit," Shepherd said without missing a beat. "Except the part about Raff claiming me. That'll happen soon, but something else needs to happen first, and you're fucking crazy if you think no one needs you. Raff still needs you and so do I."

A snort escaped Dante without his permission. "Do you really expect me to hang out on the sidelines while you two build a life together because you need me? For what? A good time?"

"No sidelines. No bullshit. I'm asking you for

everything because I love you." Shepherd dropped the words so easily—like he didn't doubt himself at all. "I was already half in love with Raff and you long before you invited me to your bed. In my wildest dreams, I never envisioned anyone like either of you wanting someone like me. You're both amazing. My whole life, I've been a failure. I didn't want to come between you." He held Dante's stare, making it impossible for Dante to call him a liar. "It was never my intention to have any part of either of you beyond that night. Knowing Raff and you had each other and were happy gave me hope. I didn't know about your world."

Dante's throat burned. Shepherd looked like a man trying to fix things, but every word he spoke made things so much worse. "Why would you tell me all this, knowing it won't change anything? Knowing there's nothing I can do about it. Now I've lost twice as much."

Shepherd stood. Dante wanted to move away. His feet wouldn't budge. Shepherd's palms slid across Dante's sides as he slowly towed him closer, as if daring Dante with his stare to pull away. "Tell me you don't feel anything for me."

Dante couldn't breathe. "Please don't do this to me."

"Then tell me," Shepherd dared. The lump in Dante's throat grew. He swallowed around it, but no words came. "Say I mean nothing."

"You know I can't," Dante choked out. "I wish I didn't feel anything. If I could close my heart, I would already be halfway around the world with three men in my bed, forgetting this town."

Shepherd walked backward while holding Dante's waist until he reached the bed. He sat and tugged Dante between his knees. His sexy green gaze never wavered from Dante's. "Stay. Before me, you never had a shot at being Raff's mate. Vampires and wolves can't form that bond, but I'm human. That doesn't apply to me. I can be a mate to either of you, or..."

Realization dawned. Dante's mind blanked. "Or both," he finished for Shepherd.

Shepherd's eyes lit. "It's only a matter of time before Raff comes looking for me. You should take advantage of this free moment to think."

Dante couldn't do more than stare at the man holding him. What Shepherd offered was everything, and he didn't know how to feel. The temptation to hope for the first time in weeks pressed in on him. They could be together. He wouldn't be the outsider.

"You should kiss me while you think things over and we wait for Raff to burst in here like the alpha he is." Shepherd's fingers stroked the small of Dante's back.

"What if I say no?"

"I'll be sad, but I won't force you to kiss me."

Dante shook his head. "That's not what I meant. What if I say no to this idea of yours?"

Shepherd's eyes darkened. "Don't ask me that."

"I have to know," Dante pressed. "If I say no, will you let me go? Will you promise to accept Raff as your mate and never think of me again?"

Shepherd shook his head. "You don't want to hear this, Dante. Don't ask me this."

Dante couldn't stop. "Tell me."

"If it's not the three of us, I'll set everyone free."

A growl escaped Dante. "Why have you still not learned that's not an option? Raff will never be free. He'll always feel the loss of you if you're not together."

"Not if I'm dead."

Dante swore he heard his heart shatter. "What?" Even to his ears, Dante sounded as if he'd been punched in the throat.

"Raff hasn't claimed me. If I should pass before then, he'll be free. It's okay." Shepherd rubbed the small of Dante's back, as if trying to comfort him. "I'm okay. No one really dies. We just move on." Shepherd blinked as if fighting back the pain. "This life, it hasn't been kind to me. When it comes to Raff and you, I won't pick a side or tear you apart. You don't do that to people you love." Something warm rolled down Dante's cheek. Shepherd wiped it away. "Don't cry. I don't want you to think about me. Think about yourself and choose what's best for you. Please don't make this about me. I won't suffer. Stryph will simply take me away. Just like walking into a dream."

"Stryph doesn't love you," Dante argued.

A small smile touched Shepherd's lips. "Oh, sweet baby. No one does. I've only ever been good enough to fuck. That's all some people get. You're still thinking of me first. Stop. In fact, I won't rush you." Shepherd stood, leaving Dante no other choice but to take a step back. He pressed a light kiss to the corner of Dante's mouth. "I'll go," Shepherd whispered against his skin.

Dante's heart did a flip in his chest at the sensation. He dragged Shepherd's scent into his lungs. "You're wrong." The words left Dante in a rush. Shepherd froze with his gaze locked on Dante. Dante could feel him holding his breath. He wouldn't make Shepherd ask. "You're wrong," he repeated. "I love you." That was the whole problem, wasn't it? When Shepherd marked Raff, Dante hadn't lost one person. He'd lost two. Dante had lost the endless possibilities of what they could become together.

Shepherd looked so hopeful, butterflies stirred in Dante's stomach. "You should definitely kiss me, then," Shepherd whispered.

Without thought, Dante shuffled closer. His hands slid up Shepherd's hard chest, savoring the way Shepherd's body felt beneath his palms. His feet kept shifting forward until there was no space between them. Dante's arms encircled Shepherd's neck. He held the man's stare, swearing he could already taste Shepherd. Shepherd broke. His mouth came down on Dante's while his fingers curled around the ends of Dante's hair. He tugged, forcing Dante's head back. Dante went hard at the rough treatment. Shepherd nipped at his lips and kissed deep. Their tongues stroked and explored. Dante kissed a path from Shepherd's lips to his jaw. The man's pulse beat against his tongue as Dante licked down his neck. His fangs scraped Shepherd's throat.

"Goddamn, I love the way that feels. Keep going."

At Shepherd's plea, Dante didn't hesitate. Blood filled his mouth as his fangs punctured the skin with ease. Shepherd's fingers dug into Dante's back as he fought to get closer. Dante could feel Shepherd's erection pressed between them. They were always explosive.

"I'm feeling pretty left out right now."

Dante licked the wound closed and pulled away. His gaze found Raff. With his arms crossed over his chest and leaned against the closed bedroom door, Raff watched them. He didn't look jealous. Dante had known he wouldn't.

With one arm wrapped around Dante's waist, Shepherd made room for Raff and held his free arm open for him. "You shouldn't. We've been waiting for you."

Raff's mouth lifted in one corner. "Are you sure? Not that I mind playing the voyeur, but this doesn't look like waiting to me."

Dante buried his face against Shepherd's chest, fighting his happiness. It was possible Raff wouldn't agree to this plan. Everything could still fall apart.

"We needed to talk some things through. You should get over here before we decide to make you watch for the hell of it."

Raff pushed away from the door. His smirk made

Dante's heart beat even faster. "I'm definitely in, but I also want to know what you've been plotting without me."

His mischievous expression was catching. Dante pressed his cheek to Shepherd's chest and joined the fun. "Kiss us and we'll tell you all about how Shepherd plans to make our dreams come true."

Shepherd tugged his hair, forcing Dante's chin up. Their gazes locked. "Is that a yes? Are you telling me yes right now?"

The massive amount of hope in Dante's chest scared the hell out of him. "If Raff still wants me, then yes."

"Yes!" Shepherd squeezed Dante to his chest and lifted him from his feet.

Raff towed them against him, joining in. "Seriously, what's this shit about '*if he still wants me*'? My nerves are gone. I'm a little irritable. It's been a long two days of chasing people. The last few weeks have been even longer. I couldn't love two people more, but it's time to quit toying with me. What the hell is going on?"

Shepherd glanced at Dante and winked. "You heard the man. He couldn't love two people more." His gaze slid back Raff's way. "That's a good thing, since you'll soon be stuck with us both."

Dante felt Raff's muscles stiffen, as if he was scared to move. "I don't... understand," Raff said, obviously picking his words carefully, as any smart man would.

"Stryph gave me the time and freedom I needed to think. He also knows all the loopholes of your world. Having his thoughts mixed with mine gave me lots of insight I didn't have before."

"That doesn't mean you're off the hook for disappearing with him," Raff said, interrupting Shepherd.

Shepherd nodded. "Yeah, later. Right now, I'm trying to say, it has to be both of you or neither of you. I'll never be happy with coming between you." A sad smile passed over Shepherd's features, melting Dante's heart. Raff's stare never budged from Shepherd. "But I also realize, I'll never be happy away from either of you. It was eating me alive, trying to figure out why I couldn't accept what a higher power had obviously deemed to be my life. Then Stryph pointed out how I don't think of one of you without including the other. He found it odd. I didn't, because if I'm being honest, I've always known I'm in love with both of you." He heard Shepherd take a bracing breath. Dante clung to every word because he knew Shepherd spoke from the heart. Shepherd was mortal. Yet he was braver than Dante or Raff. "I have to know you're together," Shepherd said, sounding like he wouldn't be moved. "Even if I'm not in the picture. But since I am, I'm the only person who can give each of you the one thing you've been missing. A true mate."

Raff sat on the bed as if his legs gave out. Dante couldn't make his fingers unclench from where they held tight to Shepherd's t-shirt, but Raff's expression swelled his throat. Dante's gaze moved over the amber eyes and the rugged good looks of the man he'd spent so many years with. He'd never seen Raff look the way he did now. Raff visibly swallowed. He blinked, as if all his emotions ruled him.

"You should probably say something," Shepherd said, sounding unsure.

Raff shook his head. "I've never been more speechless." His hands lifted before falling back to his lap as if he had nothing. He swallowed again. "This is more than I deserve. Seriously, I didn't earn this, and..." He shook his head. "I didn't earn you," Raff said, sounding pained. "The only immortals who get two mates are the selfless, because three is such a powerful number in our world. In all my life, I've never done a single thing to deserve either of you, much less both. Mated or not, one day you'll realize I'm not worthy of this, and you'll hate me."

A loud cackle escaped Shepherd. Dante's gaze snapped to Shepherd's. His eyes were an eerie light gray. Dante took a step back. He was no longer staring at Shepherd. It was Shepherd's body, but that was all. The stranger inside Shepherd's shell swiped at his eyes, wiping away tears of mirth.

"Jesus fucking Christ. I can't take another second of this. Why does Shepherd want you?"

"Stryph?" Raff asked, coming to his feet.

Stryph bowed. "The one and only. I have to say, when I brought Shepherd here, I fully intended to hand him over to you two. Oh my god, I'm glad I stuck around. Shepherd deserves so much more than this crock of shit I'm witnessing today. Now you," Stryph said, pointing at Dante. "I understand you. You genuinely love Shepherd. It's no wonder it cut Shepherd so deeply when I offered to take him away from you. But you," Stryph said, turning to Raff. "For fuck's sake, why? You didn't want him when he was all he had to offer. Then he finds a way to give you a side piece too and still you just whine, bitch, and moan." Stryph waved his arms wildly. "It's sickening."

"Let Shepherd go." The growl in Raff's voice let

Dante know the wolf was half a second from appearing.

"Why?" The taunt in that single word couldn't be missed. "Will you sack up and claim him if I do? Doubtful," Stryph said, answering his own question.

"I said, let Shepherd go." Dante took a step closer as he made the demand.

"Or what? Will you rip your mate to shreds to get to me? Maybe you'll break wolf and bite me. Of course, if you do, you might accidentally end up claiming your mate, and god fucking forbid that happen."

"He belongs to me." The alpha growl got deeper by the second. Raff's features were already becoming more animalistic.

Stryph's eyebrows rose. "I disagree. I'd say, right now, he belongs to me. Look at him." Stryph ran his hands down Shepherd's body. Dante's claws grew. His nostrils flared. Stryph didn't flinch. He kept talking as if Raff's fury meant nothing. "He's perfect, especially on the inside. If you could hear the smile in his thoughts, wow. It's just light and love in here. He's a true example of what humans were created to be." Stryph's features hardened. "Then you crash your way into his mind and you trample everything good. It was cruel of Celeste to fate him to you. He's nothing more than a pawn in a scheme, allowing you two to finally become mates after all these years. That's it and it's bullshit," Stryph said, sounding enraged. "He deserves someone who loves him. Someone who wants him for him, and not for what he can do for you. Yet all he wants is for you to be the alpha you are and step up like a real man. Good god. Pull his hair and make him go home, and for the love of all things holy, keep him safe. Has he not given you enough?"

Stryph gave voice to Shepherd's inner rage, bringing it to life. Dante could feel every word he spoke—like they cut into his soul with a knife. When they'd met Shepherd, they'd known life had been unusually cruel to him. He'd needed a soft place to land, but he was the type who wouldn't accept it. A loving hand had to take him in, kicking and screaming, and make him happy—like it or not.

Dante closed the distance between them. Raff tried stopping him, but Dante shifted through space, avoiding his grasp. "Enough," Dante growled as he grabbed two handfuls of Shepherd's shirt and hauled him forward. "I want him for him," Dante said as he captured Shepherd's mouth, refusing to think of Stryph's presence at all. His fangs grew, the way they always did when they kissed. Dante pierced his own lip, letting his blood flow freely through their kiss, because Stryph was right. Shepherd needed someone to take charge. There was a tugging in his chest as their souls stitched together. Right or wrong, he'd already taken Shepherd's blood, and now the blood exchange was complete. They were blood mates. Raff's arms clamped around them, holding them in place. Dante turned his head in time to see Raff's teeth sink into Shepherd's neck. A loud gasp tore through Shepherd. His knees gave out. Only Dante and Raff kept him from crashing to the floor. Dante led Raff's wrist to Shepherd's mouth. Shepherd's eyes opened. He had one gray and one green iris as he bit into Raff's arm. The backs of Dante's eyes burned. As he looked on, Shepherd's eyes returned to their normal color.

"I love you," Dante whispered as he watched Shepherd take in Raff's blood. He knew there was a real possibility they'd just created an oncoming shit storm. They'd definitely stolen what should've been a beautiful moment from Shepherd. After swallowing Raff's blood, Shepherd pressed his cheek to Raff's forearm. He looked winded and beautiful as he held Dante's stare.

"Why are you looking at me like that?"

At Shepherd's question, Dante swallowed past the lump in his throat. "How am I looking at you?"

"Like I've grown a second head," Shepherd whispered, sounding weak.

It hit Dante. Shepherd didn't know. He didn't realize Stryph still lived inside him, controlling the hard parts of Shepherd's life. "Not a second head, no." Just a second person. "I'm worrying over your health. You took our blood. I'm not sure of the repercussions of a human drinking vampire and werewolf blood within seconds of each other."

He doesn't know.

Raff turned his head and met Dante's stare. He looked ecstatic, considering their current situation. "It worked. I heard your thoughts."

"What don't I know?" Shepherd asked, proving he'd heard Dante as well.

A smile tugged at Dante's lips. He didn't know what would happen if he told Shepherd the truth. Stryph might appear and never let go. Dante cupped Shepherd's cheek. "You don't know how much your life will change now."

Shepherd turned his head and kissed Dante's palm. "It's okay. I can learn." Obviously unconcerned, Shepherd leaned back and touched his lips to Raff's. Dante shuffled closer. He couldn't stop himself from kissing Shepherd's neck. They had some stuff that definitely needed to be addressed, but this was his mate now. He'd never thought to have one. The moment was overwhelming, and unfair to Shepherd. Claiming a mate usually included sex because it was such a powerful and intimate moment. They'd simply taken what they wanted. The backs of Dante's eyes burned. Stryph was right about them. They trampled everything good about Shepherd and it was complete bullshit.

SIX

THERE WAS A HOLLOW PIT IN SHEPHERD'S stomach. He knew he should be ecstatic. After all, he'd gotten everything he wanted. Right? Except, nothing felt right. There was something just off or missing. Maybe he'd expected that being claimed as anyone's mate would be different. Special. Instead, Dante and Raff had gone through the steps, and then it was over. They'd spent a few hours curled up together in Dante's bed. They'd kissed, and Dante had drifted off. It had been... nice. Unfortunately, not long after Dante had fallen asleep, Raff had left to check on his pack. There wasn't a chance in hell Shepherd could sleep. The sun shone bright around the edge of the blackout blinds. Not to mention, he'd gotten plenty of rest at Stryph's.

Shepherd lasted all of fifteen minutes after Raff disappeared before he rolled from the bed to wander the house. When no alarms sounded, he checked out each room. The place was huge. A few doors were closed, and Shepherd left them that way. He assumed there were more creatures sleeping he didn't want to disturb. Along his self-guided tour, Shepherd found a music room, a weapons' room, and an indoor pool. He'd stumbled into a garage with several expensive cars, which Shepherd found funny, considering he wouldn't have thought anyone there needed them. When he made it to the living room, voices floated from the kitchen and Shepherd followed the sound. Even though he had no desire to interact, it seemed it was human nature to seek out company. He spotted two men at the table. Jonathan looked different today but still recognizable. His wings were gone, and his eyes were green. Shepherd didn't have the mental capacity needed to figure that one out. He assumed just as Raff turned into a wolf and Dante's fangs weren't always visible, Jonathan sometimes looked human. The other man sitting at the table and eating pancakes was someone new to Shepherd. Long, dark, and curly hair fell over his shoulders. His eyes were two different colors, but never the same two colors. Shepherd gave him a nod as he passed.

Even though Jonathan had a book flipped up and was obviously reading, he motioned the man's way. "Lire, Shepherd. Shepherd, Lire. Lire is part of my security team."

"It's nice to meet you," Shepherd said, because he thought he should.

Lire didn't return the sentiment. "Would you like some breakfast?"

Shepherd shook his head. "Thank you, but I don't have much of an appetite." Which didn't make sense because he couldn't recall the last time he'd eaten anything at all.

"We have no sense of time around here," Jonathan said, sounding absent and obviously misinterpreting the reason for Shepherd's lack of hunger.

Shepherd could understand meals being eaten at odd times. There were too many creatures with opposing sleep schedules under one roof. In fact, a few of the people living there didn't seem to sleep at all. He was uncomfortable. Shepherd's skin felt too tight. He didn't necessarily want to be alone but neither did he feel like he belonged there. He could feel the eyes upon him, even though when he checked, no one looked his way. Shepherd headed for the back door. The all-glass door let the sunshine in. The outdoors called his name. It whispered freedom. Through the glass, Shepherd spotted a lone man sitting beneath a nearby tree. The sun shimmered against his curly blond locks, making him look like an angel. Shepherd's hand went for the door knob.

"You should stay with us."

At Lire's growled words, Shepherd glanced over his shoulder. He flashed Lire a smile. "I didn't realize I was a prisoner."

The man's mismatched gaze moved over Shepherd's features, as if he searched for something Shepherd didn't understand. "You're not, but I won't allow you near Tamil."

Jonathan patted Lire's arm. "It's okay. We have to let Tam deal with things on his own if we want him to get better."

"But," Lire began, obviously intent on arguing.

"It's fine," Jonathan repeated, cutting him off. He focused on Shepherd. "It's not you, Shepherd. Everyone here is overprotective of Tam. I hate telling anyone's business, but in this case, you need to know if you're staying here. Tam was held hostage and tortured for close to ten years. He's incredibly sweet, but he's also mentally damaged. We ask, if you go out there, that you please be mindful of that if you interact with him."

Something dark stirred in Shepherd's chest, as if Jonathan's words awoke a protective beast inside him. Shepherd nodded. "I won't upset him." But he had to go outside. Shepherd felt like his feet would take him to Tam whether Shepherd chose to go or not.

Jonathan nodded and went back to reading his book. Lire didn't look as convinced. His gaze never wavered from Shepherd. Shepherd turned away and stepped outside. He was an adult. It wasn't like he didn't know how to treat other people. Fuck, he would be glad when he could go home. If he had a home, that is. Jesus, he was mentally exhausted. As he headed Tam's way, Tam's chin lifted, and light blue eyes focused on Shepherd. He watched Shepherd's approach.

"Hi," Tam said when Shepherd was within earshot.

Shepherd smiled at the sweetness of the boy's voice. "Hi. Is it okay if I join you? It's too nice out here to stay inside."

Tam nodded. "Sure. I don't like to be inside either. I'm Tam."

"Shepherd," Shepherd said as he chose a spot a few feet away and dropped to the ground.

"I know. You don't remember, but we've met. Stryph let me bring you here to Raff." Tam made the claim while staring at the flowers he was shredding and separating into wooden bowls.

At Stryph's name, a smile popped to Shepherd's lips. "You're the first person here to say Stryph's name without an ounce of disgust."

Tamil glanced at him from beneath his lashes. "That's because he hurt Jonathan, but I know he didn't mean to. He forgets how strong he is sometimes. Stryph isn't bad." He held up a flower. "Do you know if this is lavender? All these purple blooms look the same to me. I can't tell the difference between lilacs and lavender."

Shepherd reached for it. "Here. Let me see." When Tam passed it over, Shepherd brought it to his nose and sniffed. "It's lavender," he said, handing the blooms back. "Lilac smells like perfume. Lavender has a fresher scent."

"I didn't know that," Tam said, sniffing the flowers.

Shepherd shrugged. "My mom used to grow lots of stuff when I was a kid. I liked helping her. Landry always stuck to our dad's side, and I stayed glued to my mom. I was a momma's boy." He chuckled at his admission. "So what are you making?"

"Potions. I don't remember my parents. Would you like me to make a potion for you?"

Tam looked so hopeful Shepherd couldn't say no. "Sure, but I don't know what to ask for. I've never had one."

The bright smile that lit Tam's face made Shepherd glad he'd ventured outside. "It's probably a good thing that you don't have a preference. I only know a few concoctions and six spells. I can create a draught for luck, a love potion, sleep stew, a windfall formula, poppets, and a friendship talisman. Those are the few I'm best at making, but I'm not very good at anything."

"I doubt that's true," Shepherd argued. "What's a windfall formula?"

"It helps you come into money when you're down on your luck. You don't really need that one. With two mates, you'll never want for anything. Go with the friendship talisman. You could give it to Stryph, then he won't worry so much. He'll always know you're still friends, because you can see each other any time."

Shepherd tilted his head to one side and eyed Tam. He didn't know how to respond. "I don't imagine I'll ever see Stryph again to give it to him." As he said the words, a wave of sadness rolled over him. He hadn't known Stryph long, but they'd been part of each other. Their thoughts and memories had mixed. That was closer than he'd ever been with anyone.

"That's not true. He keeps you safe."

Before Shepherd could question the statement, a black streak in the corner of his vision pulled Shepherd's attention away. A large black wolf barreled toward him. Before Shepherd had time to panic, the wolf turned into a man and skidded to a stop next to Tam. Tam giggled as grass flew into his lap. The sound was adorable and made Shepherd smile.

The dark-haired man looked to be no more than a year or two older than Tam. His blue eyes and friendly smile held Shepherd's attention.

"Hi," the new arrival said, sounding bright. He placed a loud kiss on Tamil's cheek before turning to Shepherd. "Hey, Shepherd. I'm Evan."

"Hey. You're very nude, Evan." Shepherd wasn't a prude by any definition of the word. It just seemed odd to be sitting in the bright light of day with a naked guy half his age.

Tam and Evan both laughed, sounding exactly

like they found Shepherd's words hilarious. "You're mated to the Southeast pack alpha. Surely you know wolves don't wear clothes," Tam said through his laughter.

Pants flew past Shepherd's head and hit Evan in the chest before Shepherd could think of a response.

"Cover yourself, pup," Raff growled as he settled onto the ground next to Shepherd. Shepherd bit the inside of his cheek to stop himself from smiling. He loved that possessive note to Raff's voice. No one had ever been proud to be with him, much less jealous. When Shepherd looked Raff's way, he found himself overwhelmed. Raff hauled him against his side and captured his mouth. There was a tiny voice in the back of Shepherd's head saying they should rein themselves in with people watching. Raff didn't seem to have the same concerns. His teeth sank into Shepherd's bottom lip and tugged. A moan rose in Shepherd's throat. He swallowed the sound down before it escaped. By the time Raff pulled away, Shepherd's face bloomed with heat, especially when he noticed Tam and Evan openly watching them. The pair wore matching smiles.

Evan was the first to break. "Awwww, you two are so cute. I want to pinch your cheeks."

A very wolf-like growl came from the back of Raff's throat.

Evan held up his hands in surrender. "I won't. Don't worry. So, what's everyone been doing while I was on patrol?"

"I'm making a talisman for Shepherd. He smells like Landry."

A surprised chuckle escaped Shepherd. "Okay. Well, he is my baby brother."

Tam kept his gaze locked on his hands. He was braiding some sort of twine. "I like Landry. He helps scared kids and gives them my dolls."

Shepherd worked his way through that one, surmising Tam meant because Landry was a police officer. He wondered how much Tam understood about the human world. "Any friend of my brother's is a friend of mine."

At his statement, Tam froze and glanced up at Shepherd from beneath his lashes. "That's a nice thing to say." Tam's gaze shot toward the house. A blush bloomed on his cheeks. "I'm sorry. I'll have to finish your talisman later. Risk is looking for me."

Shepherd didn't know who Risk was, but Evan laughed. "You'd better hurry. You know how much he hates it when you sneak away while he's sleeping. Mates miss their cuddle buddies."

Tam's blush deepened as he stood and headed for the house. A smile pulled at Shepherd's lips. He wondered who the lucky bastard was that won Tam. The man had to be amazing. Raff's palm slid across the small of Shepherd's back. His head emptied of all thoughts as his brain latched on to the sensation. His stomach growled, but he wasn't hungry for food.

Evan's nose hit the air and a loud groan escaped him. "Ugh. That crazy deer shifter is back. I'm sorry, guys. I have to go take care of this. Stupid deer. I'm tired of telling him to move along." Evan stood.

Shepherd's interest was piqued. "Why don't you get some of your wolf buddies together and mark the area you don't want the deer to cross. He should steer clear of the scent of dominant animals."

"You'd think," Evan said, sounding tired. "Unfortunately, he's a perverted old deer who likes to be scolded. If I pissed right on him, he'd probably come back for more. I think I'll call Bleidd to take care of it... again. See you later," Evan called over his shoulder as he headed off toward the brush.

Shepherd chuckled as he watched him go. "I'm having a hard time picturing a deer with fetishes." The final word came out in a gasp as Raff crowded his space and kissed his neck. His tongue stroked the scar he'd left on Shepherd's throat.

"When I slipped away to make sure pack business was covered in my absence, I'd hoped you would still be waiting in bed when I got back."

"I couldn't hang out in bed, staring at the ceiling any longer," he admitted as he tilted his chin up to give Raff better access to his neck. Damn, he loved the sensation of Raff's tongue on his skin.

"Oh yeah," Raff said, holding out his hand to Shepherd. "I found this while cutting through the woods. It made me think of you."

Shepherd reached for the small stone Raff held out for him. It was shaped like a heart. Shepherd rubbed it between his thumb and forefinger. It was smooth and warm from Raff holding it. "Thank you." Shepherd swallowed. His chest ached. "If I asked you a question, would you be honest with me and to hell with my feelings?"

"I don't know if I can disregard your feelings, but I'll be honest."

Shepherd kept his gaze locked on the stone. He took a breath, reaching deep for his courage. "You don't love me the way you should, do you? I mean, not like it takes to be truly tied to someone forever."

Raff ran his knuckles down Shepherd's jaw. "Why would say that?"

Try as he might, Shepherd still couldn't lift his

chin to meet Raff's gaze. He touched his chest, holding the stone against his beating heart. "Because I feel it here. I think you care about me as much as you would any fated mate, but it's not the passionate love you feel for someone you spend your life with."

Raff moved even closer. His voice turned soft and pleading. "I wish you'd tell me what I've done to make you feel this way."

Shepherd felt ridiculous. He didn't know how to explain the way he felt. It wasn't in his nature to show his heart. He swiped his palms on his thighs. "It's not important. Forget I said anything."

Raff stood. He held his hand out for Shepherd. "Come with me."

Shepherd took Raff's hand and allowed the man to pull him to his feet. With their fingers linked, Raff led Shepherd inside. They didn't encounter a soul as Raff made his way to an empty bedroom. He closed them inside and faced off against Shepherd.

"I failed you last night. You deserved to have me make love to you as I claimed you."

"It's okay," Shepherd said out of habit.

"No. It's not," Raff argued, sounding angry on Shepherd's behalf. He dragged his fingers down Shepherd's chest. "I remember the first moment I saw you like it happened today. Every second of every day since, I've fought the urge to drop everything and run to you. It's been hell, because I know if I'd shown up on your doorstep, you would've thought badly of me, since you've never stopped insisting I belong with Dante. I'd rather rip out my heart than have you look at me with disgust." Raff paused and visibly swallowed. "Outside, just now, I'm convinced if you'd turned your head and looked my way, I would've seen that disgust I've feared."

"No."

At his denial, Raff went flush against him. The moment their bodies met, Shepherd felt Raff go hard. "Tell Stryph to take a break so you can prove me wrong."

"What?" Even Shepherd heard the confusion in his voice.

"I don't want him," Raff said, not backing down. "If he wants to hang around and keep you safe when Dante and I aren't around to do so, I can live with that. I can feel how much you matter to him, but he needs to leave for this."

"I don't un—" The words died on Shepherd's lips as smoke rose from his skin, solidifying into Stryph's form across the room. "How... I don't understand."

"Hello, beautiful angel."

Shepherd blinked. "You've been here the whole time?"

Stryph didn't look the least bit contrite. He clasped his hands behind his back. "I'm keeping my promise to fix your life."

Shepherd wanted to be upset, but he understood Stryph. They understood each other. For different reasons, they were a lot alike. Shepherd had spent his life lonely because he'd been meant for Raff. Stryph had been deeply lonely for more years than Shepherd could fathom because he was meant for no one. He wasn't a soul to have another half. He'd been created as a tool to keep balance. His happiness had never factored.

Raff kissed his cheek. "When you're ready, Dante and I will be waiting for you." His lips brushed Shepherd's ear. "And, for the record, I absolutely do love you passionately. It's been hell waiting to have you alone."

Shepherd took a deep breath, trying to cool his reaction to the heat in Raff's voice. There was the intensity he'd been missing. Their hands clung until the last second as Raff walked away, leaving him alone with Stryph.

When Shepherd focused on Stryph, Stryph's

mouth lifted in one corner in a wicked smile. "Alone at last, sexy."

Shepherd ignored Stryph's flirting. "Why have you stayed hidden? If Raff knew you were here, why would you hide from me?" Shepherd couldn't hide the hurt in his voice. He'd thought they'd never see each other again and Stryph had been right there the whole time.

"Awww, gorgeous. I didn't want you to think of me while you chose what you wanted. It had to be your decision whether you stayed here. You deserve to make your own choices without my influence." His expression turned sad. "And I knew, if you knew I was there, you'd feel how much I believe you'd be better off with me." He tilted his head from one side to the other, obviously ready to amend his words. "Or at the very least, I would've convinced you to sweep Dante away and leave Raff behind."

Shepherd was taken aback by that response. "Why? I thought you understood I feel equally about both."

"Honestly?" Stryph asked, as if Shepherd would want him to lie. "I didn't think he loves you, but I might've been wrong. Now I'm starting to think it's just the whole alpha wolf thing. He's used to people falling in line and understanding their place. It's obvious he didn't realize, as a human, you'd need him to use his words and body to show his love. You weren't born and bred to recognize how, as his fated mate, you're always the first and last thing on his mind. It'll take time for you to accept that everything he does, every decision he makes, it's all for you."

Shepherd's throat burned. He swallowed hard at the sensation. "See? That's precisely why I need you around. You always say exactly what I need to hear." Shepherd moved a step closer. "I know I have more than my fair share now, but you're my friend. That's something I still need. You can't be hanging around inside me without my knowledge. That's not fair to Dante and Raff, but I don't want you to disappear either. You need me too." Shepherd knew Stryph wouldn't like having that last point said aloud, but it needed to be said. He'd known who Stryph was minutes after picking through the man's thoughts. Stryph was dangerous. Without anyone keeping him in check, someone to cling to, Stryph might choose to turn the world against itself to watch it burn. But there was also a deep well of love and a huge sense of justice inside Stryph. He believed good should always win in the end. Shepherd thought he was amazing.

To his surprise, Stryph smiled. "Well, you know I

can't be hanging around all day. There are other utterly lost souls out there."

Shepherd fought the urge to snort. He knew that wasn't why Stryph had chosen to help him. Stryph had spotted him inside Raff's Pool Hall. He'd felt Shepherd's longing and loneliness, and he'd seen a kindred spirit. Stryph had watched him. His curiosity eventually turned into a longing of his own. When he'd watched Shepherd make his rage-filled trek to Jonathan's for help, he'd lost the battle against approaching him. The funny thing was, if Stryph had reached out to him before Shepherd had sliced Raff with that knife, Shepherd knew in his heart he would've chosen Stryph.

A sad smile passed over Stryph's features, as if he heard Shepherd's thoughts. "I know, babe," he said, proving he heard more than Shepherd realized. "I've never had a good sense of timing." He shrugged. "Or maybe I just knew I'd make you miserable. Either way, I know I can't stay. I just wanted to see you happy before I leave."

A shot of panic hit Shepherd. "Don't leave for good. When I thought I'd never see you again, it broke my heart. I still need you."

Stryph's smile turned sweet. "You don't need

anyone, gorgeous. Haven't I taught you anything? You're so fucking strong, it's blinding."

"I need you," Shepherd repeated. "And you need me. We're friends. Probably closer to partners in crime."

The chuckle that fell from Stryph's lips was sexy as hell. "I'll be back. You know I can't stay away. Until then, you know where to find me. You're the only one who does." Stryph winked and was gone. No long goodbyes or heart-wrenching moments. He simply vanished, leaving Shepherd behind. But he wasn't gone, not really. Shepherd could still feel him. Stryph was right. He was the only person who understood he was right there, just beyond the veil, and Stryph had left all the knowledge Shepherd would need to get there inside Shepherd's head. They'd be together again soon. It was fate.

WHEN RAFF LEFT Shepherd alone with Stryph, he'd fully intended to show Stryph some trust and hope Stryph showed the same. Unfortunately, the moment he stepped into the hallway, his feet froze. He couldn't move more than five feet from the room where his mate stood with the man who'd already stolen him once. Raff paced those five feet until he thought his nerves would snap. When Shepherd stepped out, Raff's guilt over not trusting him showed in his smile.

"Hey."

Shepherd's dark expression cleared as his gaze landed on Raff. "Hey. I thought you were waiting for me in bed." His feet kept moving until he backed Raff against the wall. "Not that I'm complaining about stealing another moment alone with you."

As if his hands had a mind of their own, they snaked beneath the hem of Shepherd's shirt and stroked the man's bare skin. He nodded toward the door. "Is everything okay in there?"

Shepherd nodded. "He's gone, but we'll see each other again."

He could feel how much Shepherd cared about Stryph, so he didn't argue. "I know. How could anyone stay away from you?"

A mischievous glint entered Shepherd's eyes. "I don't know. You're doing a pretty damn good job of it."

Raff wanted to tease and drag out the moment. The beast inside him wasn't in the mood to play. Raff hauled Shepherd closer. His fingers tightened on the man's jaw as his lips found Shepherd's. The vibration at the back of his throat was the wolf, showing his satisfaction. The low growl could be felt in their kiss as their tongues stroked. Raff's teeth scraped Shepherd's bottom lip. He savored their kiss, even as his gums itched with the need to bite. Raff hadn't claimed his mate the proper way. The knowledge made his alpha side antsy.

"Did you say that bedroom was empty now?"

Shepherd nodded at his question, even as he dragged Raff in for a deeper kiss. Raff urged Shepherd backward, maneuvering him inside the bedroom. He kicked the door closed behind them. His hands found Shepherd's ass. He lifted, using his unnatural strength against the man. Raff took Shepherd down on the mattress, covering Shepherd's body with his. They tore at each other's clothes while trying not to break their kiss. The sound of material ripping filled the air. It didn't matter. Raff would buy Shepherd all the things once they were back home. With Shepherd's massive chest bare, Raff kissed a path down his body. He fucking loved the way the hair on Shepherd's torso felt against his lips. Raff let his teeth lightly scrape Shepherd's nipple before moving lower. His tongue traced Shepherd's ribs. Raff's dick strained to get closer as Raff reached the button of Shepherd's jeans. The button and zipper easily gave way beneath Raff's touch. The instant he set Shepherd's cock free, his tongue found the salty prize he'd been searching for.

Shepherd tugged at Raff's hair, pulling him closer. Raff stripped away the rest of Shepherd's clothes before allowing Shepherd to have his way. He licked and sucked even as he toyed with Shepherd's asshole. He loved that Shepherd would do anything. The man loved to get fucked every bit as much he enjoyed dishing it out. Eternity was a long time. Experimenting was everything. Raff could show him more pleasure than he'd ever dreamed.

In an unexpected move, Shepherd shoved him away and reached for Raff's zipper. He took control, stripping away the last of Raff's clothes. "You have to let me play too," Shepherd demanded as his fingers encircled Raff's shaft. Stars popped behind his eyes at the first touch of his mate. Damn, no one had warned him how over the top his every emotion would be. No one had told him his mate's touch would feel a hundred times better than anyone who'd ever touched him. In one stroke, Raff was ready to come unglued. With Raff's cock held tight in his fist, Shepherd tugged, urging him higher. "This should be in my mouth when you suck my dick."

A wolf-like growl escaped him as he went on the

attack. Shepherd's words stirred the flames. In a single move, he had Shepherd down his throat and his dick in the man's face. Shepherd dragged his tongue down Raff's length. His skin tightened, and his claws grew. Shepherd's hot mouth closed around Raff's crown. Raff sucked—hard, needing Shepherd to feel even a third of what the man did to him. Shepherd's tongue wiggled against Raff's overly sensitive nerve endings. Something inside Raff snapped. His head bobbed as he went at Shepherd with everything he had. He gave what he took. His hips rotated, openly fucking Shepherd's mouth like he took the man's ass. He fingered Shepherd as he sucked him, determined to make him insane.

Raff's balls drew up tight. His every muscle tightened. Shepherd massaged the spot between his balls and asshole as his throat tightened around Raff's dick. Hot cum filled Raff's mouth. A groan of pleasure vibrated around his cock. An explosion rocked him as jet after jet of cum pumped from him. Shepherd hummed as if he'd been given his favorite treat.

While gasping for air, Raff pulled away and rearranged their bodies until he could claim Shepherd's mouth. The taste of their fluids combined. Raff couldn't get enough. He tried licking every place he could reach inside Shepherd's mouth, seeking every drop of them. They were real. This was only the beginning. He wanted to climb so far up Shepherd's ass the man couldn't get away. The only reason it hadn't happened was because this wasn't their room. He didn't have any lube. Raff wouldn't hurt his angel.

"We should wake Dante. He could bring what we need," Shepherd said, as if he'd been in Raff's head, which he probably had. It was difficult to hide thoughts from a mate and most didn't try. Their bond was too special and vital. They made each other whole.

"Call him," Raff urged. He needed Shepherd to embrace the fact that he could, at any time, reach out with his mind and connect with them.

"I don't know how."

Raff swiped the sweat-soaked hair away from Shepherd's face and held his stare. "Yes you do. Just open your mind and call to him."

Shepherd's eyes lost focus, as if he turned inside himself. *Dante.*

Raff smiled as Shepherd's thoughts rolled over him.

We're waiting.

Bring the lube, Raff added, ensuring Dante hurried.

"You can hear me too when I talk to him?"

Raff nodded. "I can hear you always. Sometimes it's just a hum in the back of my mind, bringing me comfort. Other times, you drown out everything. Either way, I never get tired of knowing you're there."

"Goddamn. Look at all this sexiness just waiting to be ravaged," Dante said, appearing at the edge of the bed. Raff turned his head just in time to see a bottle of lube go sailing past them as it was tossed onto the mattress. Dante's green eyes were unnaturally bright. His long hair draped over one shoulder as he pushed his pajama pants down his hips. Raff rolled to the side, exposing Shepherd's nude body for Dante's delight as he made room for Dante to join them. "Yum. You're both already sticky and ready for me." Dante's palm slid across Shepherd's chest as he slipped into bed on the other side of Shepherd. "I wish I knew what I did to deserve to have so much sexiness in one bed."

"You came when I called," Shepherd said, sounding amazed. Raff's gaze shot to Shepherd. He was staring at Dante in disbelief.

Dante's features softened. "I'll always come when you need me."

Shepherd urged Dante's mouth to his. Raff's breath caught as he watched them kiss. He loved these men. It sat on his chest all hours of the day. "I'm here," Dante said so quietly Raff wouldn't have heard if he didn't have werewolf hearing. "You should definitely make love to me now." Even as Dante made the claim, he towed Raff into their kiss.

Their tongues toyed with one another as their hands roamed. Cool lube coated his cock and Raff never saw Shepherd reach for the bottle. "I'm totally going to be the greedy boy in the middle. It's been too long since I've had either of you," Shepherd said as he rolled Dante onto his stomach.

Raff tried tempering his breathing as he watched Shepherd fuck Raff with his fingers, stretching and lubing his ass. Damn, they were a sexy feast for the eyes. Dante's flushed face and the way he humped the mattress, openly seeking relief, had Raff hard and ready to go. He stroked himself as Shepherd's cock disappeared inside Dante. The sound Dante made tightened Raff's skin. Incapable of taking another second, Raff shifted onto his knees. Shepherd made room for him between his knees. Raff ran his hand down Shepherd's spine, savoring the moment as he swiped his crown against Shepherd's asshole. He pushed, slipping inside a hair before retreating. Shepherd's tight, hot ass was greedy, trying to pull him deeper. Raff surged forward again, watching as his dick slowly slid, inch by inch, inside Shepherd. A soft moan filled the room. Raff rotated his hips, trying to make it happen again. They moved in time, each straining toward the same goal. Dante's and Shepherd's thoughts crowded his brain, even as his pleasure grew. It was overwhelming. Even having just orgasmed only minutes earlier, Raff didn't know how long he'd last. He'd never expected this. Three parts making one whole and he was one big nerve. Every sensation was mind-blowing. He rocked and pumped, taking his pleasure and seeking more. Pressure climbed up his shaft and beat at his crown. Moans vibrated from his throat as the wolf clawed at Shepherd's skin, leaving marks down his sides and back. Possessiveness ruled his every action.

I love you.

Shepherd's thoughts caressed Raff's brain, bringing him even closer to the edge.

I love you both so much I can't breathe.

The confession sent Raff flying. Lights popped behind his eyes. Love choked him. Wave after wave of ecstasy rocked his soul.

"Goddamn, I love you," Raff whispered against Shepherd's back as he fought for air. "I'll make you feel it." It was a vow Raff planned to keep. He knew Shepherd would need time to see inside Raff the way Raff saw inside him. Raff wouldn't stop until they were all so on top of one another in their minds, Dante and Shepherd begged for peace. This was love. He'd prove it.

SEVEN

Shepherd sat at a table in the corner of Raff's Pool Hall, holding the poppet and friendship talisman Tamil had made for him. It had been three months since Raff, Dante, and he had been living under one roof. It had been the best three months of his life, doubly so since Landry was now his neighbor. He loved seeing his brother almost every day. Still, Stryph was a hole missing in his chest. Shepherd knew he could go visit, but he was nervous. Since Stryph hadn't sought him out, he worried their friendship was over. Shepherd had never been good at letting people go.

Raff and Dante had urged him to find Stryph. Instead, he'd gone to visit Tam and gotten these gifts. He stared down at the doll and the leather and twine keychain. Even though he'd been born human, he could still feel the power surging from the items. His eyes stung. It was ridiculous that he cared as much as he did. Shepherd had always been that way. Everyone hated the man who'd been his best friend for years, Frankie. Shepherd hadn't once given up on him, even though Frankie was an ass more often than not. Of course, nowadays, they didn't see each other much. Not since Frankie had miraculously decided to do right by his wife and stay home. Still, Shepherd valued the people in his life.

Warm lips touched the top of his head as hands landed on his shoulders. Shepherd knew without looking they belonged to Raff. He could tell the difference between his mates' touch, even in the dark. "Go see him," Raff said, sounding exactly like he'd said the same words a hundred times, because he had. "My truck is sitting outside. Go."

"I'm still thinking it over," Shepherd confessed.

"Ugh, I can't take it," Stryph said, appearing in the seat beside Shepherd and nearly causing his heart to fail. "I want my presents and you're just taking forever to work through this self-doubt, sexy. Jesus."

Shepherd was too happy to see Stryph to care what he said. "I knew you were there," he lied, stirring the pot. "I wondered how long it would take you to break."

Raff snorted and kissed Shepherd on the head again. "Behave, boys. I have pack business."

Shepherd watched his man go with lust in his heart. Damn, his alpha looked hot in a form-fitting pair of jeans. "I'll be good."

"Liar," Stryph breathed in a stage whisper. "Give me. Give me," he said, wiggling his fingers at Shepherd and immediately forgetting to play with Raff.

"You're like a giant child. Tell me why you haven't been to see me, and you can have your gifts. I'm not giving them up until then."

Stryph huffed. "Sometimes I have to work. The world doesn't destroy itself, you know. Plus, you needed some alone time with your new mates. You don't get to be newly mated forever. I figured you'd want to enjoy it without your fairy godmother hanging around."

Mildly satisfied with Stryph's excuse, Shepherd handed the gifts to Stryph. "Tam says the poppet is for protection, which I don't figure you'll need, but he weaved some of my love for you inside as well." Stryph's expression made his slight embarrassment worthwhile. He visibly swallowed as he stared at the tiny doll without blinking. Shepherd kept talking. "Also, I know you can find me anytime you want, but I have to work to get to you. Tam says, if you're willing, all you have to do is kiss the keychain. That'll complete the spell, and then all I have to do is touch the keychain to any mirror to make that mirror a doorway to you. He says Evan already uses one to visit him. Oh, and don't worry. If I lose it, it won't be of any use to anyone else. Tamil says it's powered by the strength of our friendship. That's why it's called a friendship talisman. Obviously," Shepherd added, because he couldn't stop rambling. He pressed his lips together, hoping to stifle the nervous chatter.

Stryph met his stare. As he held Shepherd's gaze, Stryph brought the keychain to his lips. He held the talisman against his mouth, as if making Shepherd a silent promise. "I'd be honored to have you as a bigger part of my life," Stryph said, handing the keychain back to Shepherd. "Please use it." His expression changed, turning wicked. "Just announce yourself when you stop by, because you know I have... peculiar tastes."

It took every ounce of Shepherd's will not to blush and fan his face. He knew. "Um, yeah. I remember."

An evil-sounding chuckle fell from Stryph's lips.

He straightened and tucked the poppet in his shirt pocket, right over his heart. "Now, you have one mate sleeping and one hosting a pack meeting. That gives us a few hours. What trouble shall we start?" Before Shepherd could come up with an idea, Stryph's face brightened. "I know. If you plan to start traveling via the mirror world, I should show you how. Let's go visit with Tam and Evan. Those two are lowkey mischief makers by day, every day."

Shepherd couldn't picture it, but he loved the idea of visiting Tam. He also couldn't wait to try out the mirror thing, or to spend the day with Stryph. Hell, the whole rest of his life was looking up. With Stryph at his side and Dante and Raff as his mates, Shepherd had never felt more blessed. All he needed now was to find someone slightly twisted and extra perverted for Stryph to spend eternity with, and Shepherd would be complete.

Keep an eye out for the next Hellish book.

Please consider leaving a review at the retailer where this book was purchased. Reviews really help with a book's visibility, which ensures I can continue writing. Thank you, Charity.

ABOUT THE AUTHOR

Charity Parkerson is an award winning and multi-published author with several companies. Born with no filter from her brain to her mouth, she decided to take this odd quirk and insert it in her characters.

*Seven-time Readers' Favorite Award Winner
   *2015 Passionate Plume Award Finalist
   *2013 Reviewers' Choice Award Winner
   *2012 ARRA Finalist for Favorite Paranormal Romance
   *Five-time winner of The Mistress of the Darkpath

Connect with her online:

--Join my street team: facebook.com/TeamCharityParkerson
   --Sign up for my newsletter: http://bit.ly/CharityNews

--Website: charityparkerson.com

--Facebook:

facebook.com/authorCharityParkerson

facebook.com/TheMenofSin

--Twitter: twitter.com/CharityParkerso